T0194169

A NOCTURNE OF ECHOES

A NOCTURNE OF ECHOES

CAYDEN CARRICO

A NOCTURNE OF ECHOES

iUniverse books may be ordered through booksellers or by contacting:

iUniverse
1663 Liberty Drive
Bloomington, IN 47403
www.iuniverse.com
1-800-Authors (1-800-288-4677)

ISBN: 978-1-4917-4493-2 (sc)
ISBN: 978-1-4917-4495-6 (hc)
ISBN: 978-1-4917-4494-9 (e)

Library of Congress Control Number: 2014915621

Print information available on the last page.

iUniverse rev. date: 11/19/2018

PROLOGUE

S queezed just between two ridges, a long, green clearing cut through the maple forest around it. Stone walls encircled and fortified the clearing barring any trespassers from violating the sovereignty of the estates boundaries. Paths leading through the surrounding gardens sprawled across the estate, centralizing to the northernmost corner leading up to the grand steps of the palace, North Haven. Snuggled inside the crescent of the northern ridge, North Haven sat atop a small foothill at the its base, gazing over its domain. It dominated the horizon from high above its hill, eclipsing even the sun for most of the day.

North Haven, whose main building was adjoined on both of its sides by two wings, barely fit on the modest hill it was constructed upon. Stone walls had been tasked to hold up such a colossal monument but teetered inward from disrepair. Two rows of windows ran parallel across the face of the home, allowing a distorted glimpse of inside through shattered glass. The three outstretching wings culminated toward a center rotunda, the entrance, that all roads led to. There sat two doors that had been sealed for a little more than half a century, separating heaven on earth from the rest of the world.

This forgotten palace had lived the life of a song, whimsically and carelessly following each measure of its existence, bound to a simple melody that grew and evolved through its lifetime. The changes were subtle with each passing day, but the differences grew appreciably greater over the years as each new generation of residents deviated from the original score. Here was offered the greatest escape—to live life in heaven, to run into lovers, a place to marry and start new beginnings, only to watch it all fall apart. Here was offered freedom—to make mistakes to run away from, to end a journey, and then to live only for a delusional glimpse of past glory.

A heritor and exemplar of some past misbegotten fortune, North Haven had once been something to admire. But it had never been a home to anyone. Between the sway of the home's life and grandeur, selfish indifference festered, the kind that would hollow out any sort of family that had once lived in its vast halls.

CHAPTER 1

A Place for Ghosts

Jordan remembered seeing the house as she came over the pass, a lumbering palace crouching just below the tallest trees. Finally, within sight of her destination, she forgot about the aches and pains from the past ten-hour hike and picked up her pace. Everything she needed for a two-day expedition was packed on her back.

She had discovered the abandoned estate a few years back on a hunting trip with her father. Back then, she had asked her father if they could go check it out and explore this hidden wonder of the world; naturally his response had been a swift no. Every year after that, they would run into the mysterious palace, and every year, Jordan would become more and more intrigued. Staying away from the mysterious castle probably was for the best but, the potential danger could never hold back her curiosity and by the time she'd moved out of her dad's home to start her own life, she had made it her mission to see what was really going on in the old place.

Now the house loomed in the near distance, just a silhouette of gray bricks filling in the space between the trees. She got to the clearing in the woods where the home's stone perimeter walls held back the encroaching forest from the rest of the estate. It was from there that she could fully see the scope of the estate. Distance had hidden its flaws, as the promising palace had been rubble all along. Time, with its erosive force, had taken the place from grace, twisting and warping it into something less remarkable than.

High above the ground, a red tile roof stretched across the upper facing of the home. Quarried, mortared limestone bricks formed the walls and held up the palace, each spaced apart from each other by ornate ones chiseled with wreaths, and ferns. The home stood as tall as it could manage against the overbearing weight of neglect. Ivy reached up like hands assailing the walls as it wormed its way through the mortar between the stone. Those red tiles had been racked and weathered as they attempted to hold their place from the years of rain.

A haunting silence followed her through the estate's front terrace as she continued down the trail. Two arched windows bordered a single door that marked the end of the trail. Jordan walked through the clearing and toward the door along a dirt trail that seamlessly became a paved path. She stepped up to the door, which was flanked on both sides by two lanterns. Jordan stood in front of the door, her hand reluctant to pull the door's handle. She almost preferred to knock. It was now that she had begun to doubt her decision to come, but with a little reassurance and a reminder of the arduous hike up here, she convinced herself to open the door. It creaked open slowly in a dramatic fashion to a gaping foyer that receded back into two unlit corridors. Before her, a grand hall sprawled out indefinitely, paved by marble tiles paled by years of gathered dust. Crafted wooden framework lined the lower halves of the walls, while the upper half was covered by the remains of beige wallpaper, now curled and tattered. Above her, she could see a balcony encircling the top half of the foyer, its railing possessed same intricate design of the woodwork. She took two aimless steps as her head pivoted in all directions unable to take in the full glory of the ruin.

She noticed two staircases at both sides of her and then the two halls that diverged off in the back. A few steps toward the entrance of the hallway left her just as far away from the end as when she had started. She smiled to herself, feeling some sense of fulfillment for her trespassing. Her sense of wonder had started to outweigh her worry, drawing her further into the home. Without any sense of purpose, Jordan strayed off into the far-right hallway, staying on the first floor. Countless doors lining either side of the halls accounted for her growing wonder. There was so much to see and so much to appreciate, Jordan didn't know where to begin. She wanted to get a glimpse of everything before she gave any of it a considerable look. After all, she was going to be here for a couple of days and there was no need to rush anything now.

One random turn after the next led her to a long corridor that ran across the back of the home. Windows that towered over her, lined the entire east facing of the home and showered her in the light of a mid-summer's sunset as she entered the hall. She looked beyond the glare to a panoramic view of the back lawn. She continued along the hall with her eyes fixed at the end of the hall where the ceiling, floor and walls converged to one point. Her solitude followed her as the noiseless environment amplified each step, reminding her of her detachment from the rest of the world.

Her wandering ended when the hall she had followed came to an end at a single door. There was no point in backtracking, so naturally, she opened the door to whatever lay on the other side. A strong draft grabbed the door forcing her to pull it harder than she had expected. Beyond it was a gaping cavity that could have easily been mistaken for the night sky. Jordan pulled out and waved her flashlight around in the expanse of the dark void. The light from her flashlight diminished as it traveled the distance of the room, fading into a dull glow that barely touched the far walls. She shined it at a lower angle, revealing seats aligned in a descending fashion and walkways between large columns of aisles, all set facing a stage, a massive room used as a relatively small auditorium. The outside was deceiving. It wasn't that the auditorium was large; even her high school had a larger auditorium, but rather that the home even had one.

She stepped in and waved her flashlight around to fully see the scope of thispreserved auditorium, its beam darting to each corner of the room. There must have been auditorium held at least two hundred seats, all covered with red velvet fabric held together by a cast-iron frameRust and dust consumed the theatre; the once beautiful red curtains had now been superimposed with a layer of dust fading it to an unremarkable brown. The cast-iron seats were covered with a golden patina that interlaced the darkened iron. The auditorium had corroded away into this blighted brown this color of decay, neglect, and death.

She smiled to herself, feeling both astonished and incredulous at the idea that someone would want to leave this all behind. And if there was an auditorium, what else might have been abandoned in this big, empty house?

* * *

The tide of dusk began to veil the sunlit sky, whose bright cobalt diminished into a deep, ultramarine blue. The forest beyond the home's walls became motionless and still, with only lifeless silhouettes of branches and foliage rising above the border, like hands reaching over, grasping the walls. The home's empty halls echoed an unsettling silence, complimented by the empty rooms that added to its lifeless void. Outside of the sparse light that Jordan's lamp offered, the inside had fallen to an augmented darkness. Exterior light was blocked out by the home's concealing walls, and all that kept the home from reaching pitch-black was the extrinsic light that poured in from the colonnade of windows that lined almost every hall.

Jordan had taken a moment to stare out the window as she unpacked her thing. She'd chosen this room out of convenience since it was the closest to the stair case and after the exhausting climb up the stairs, she didn't want to walk any farther. The owners left nothing left in the room except for its emptiness. It looked like it had once been someone's office. The room was small; obviously, it hadn't belonged to anyone important. But that didn't take away from its significance. She set all her things down being less interested in carrying anything and more interested in exploring.

Less than ten minutes of wandering through random rooms and halls had taken her to the house's library. She'd figured there would be one in such a big house. Why wouldn't there be one? Whether or not the owners read didn't really change the fact that a library and dozens of other needless rooms would be needed to fill such a place. She had been sitting at one of the desks flipping through an old encyclopedia indexed for the letter *E*. Discoloration from age on each page discredited whatever valid knowledge might still be left in the book. It was becoming too late to read. And after such a long day it was easy to call it a night. She opened the library door to a long, unwelcoming dark corridor that seemed to swallow the light of her flashlight as she shined it down the protracted hall.

Each step she took felt like a risk as she walked through the darkness. Nothing felt certain except for the imagined dangers that her mind assured her were in every dark corner. She walked by one of the many intermittently placed doors that lined this hall before stopping suddenly when she heard the sound of something besides her own footsteps. A slow, methodical tick cut through the silence and echoed from a room to her left. She stood still and listened for a moment; each tick felt like a small taunt. In disbelief, she tried to ignore her imagination and continue down the hall, but the unnatural tick was just too much to ignore.

She pointed her flashlight toward the door and faced the room, being careful not to step inside. The ticking was gone. She surveyed the room with her flashlight, trying to find the source.

Two small desks faced the front of the room towards a wheeled chalkboard. And then she saw it. On the floor lay a motionless clock. Feeling reassured, she tiptoed across the room and picked up the clock, its hands frozen at just before eleven fifteen. Its white marble face was laminated in dust. Its glass cracked down the front. The nail that it once hung from was still attached to its back. She now looked toward the wall beside it and saw a small hole. Then she looked back at the clock.

The walls seethed with shadows that festered behind her in the growing darkness, that were careful to not stray into the light—shadows that had festered longer than the clock's existence. Jordan looked at the clock, now hanging from the wall. It was still dead and broken but not completely worthless. And she felt a sense of fulfillment; she forced a smile at the minute restoration.

Her return to her room was all but pleasant. She knew no one else was here with her and wasn't one to believe in the supernatural, but she couldn't help but feel as if the origninal owners were still here. It seemed that whoever had lived here had spent far too much money on the place for someone like her to stay here.

CHAPTER 2

Escape to Paradise

On the murky day of November 12, 1930, light gleamed through the thick, overcast sky covering Manhattan into Eugene Motter's office window, which overlooked the city from its twelve-story perch. Eugene Motter sat facing the window, feeling snug and secure as he stared out at the downpour, his bloated body fitting snuggly in the chair that was barely able to contain him. He was wearing the finest blue suit that the world could tailor, and he took great pride and pleasure in being the best dressed around the office. After all, he was the boss. When an expected knock at the door caught his attention, Eugene turned around, composing himself in a professional manner.

"Come in," Eugene replied.

"You wanted to see me, Mr. Motter?" The young businessman said timidly, his body quivering behind the cover offered by the door with only his head halfway in the room. He knew what was coming.

"Yes, I wanted to discuss your recent performance and how we might deal with it," said Eugene, and he flipped through some paperwork on his desk. The young man hung over his boss's words earnestly until the silence ate away at what was left of his optimistm.

"And …" the young man stuttered.

"You're wasting my money.'" Eugene snarled, a malicious look overtaking his once almost professional-looking face. "You're investing in frivolous bonds that were declining when you bought them. Do you know how asinine that is? You're disgracing me and my firm!"

"I can explain!" said the man.

"You don't need to explain why you're fired. I already know," Eugene said unsympathetically.

"But what about my family?" the man wailed. "I'll never find another job now."

"What about *your* family? I have a family too that I need to take care of. You don't see me wasting money. Maybe you should have been more cautious."

"But … my family, we'll end up on the streets if I don't keep my job," the man pleaded. But in truth, he had already conceded to his own error and, thus, was unable to make any sort of stand.

"Much better you than I," Eugene said as he dismissed the broken businessman out the door.

Discarded and defeated, the man shamefully slid out the door as quickly as he had come through them. Eugene spun around in his chair to face the window and let out a huge sigh as if he had just been fired, a sigh for his lost assets. He couldn't imagine why incompetence ravaged his firm so much lately.

At the end of another long day, Eugene stood outside his office holding an umbrella as he waited for his chauffer. He looked around to see that beggars choked the street with their pestilence. He gave each one a look of disgust and shook his head. How dare they loiter in front of his firm. When his ride had finally arrived to take him home, he looked one last time at the destitute masses that overran the city. It had been a couple of years since the stock market crash, complicating everything he ever knew. Running his firm seemed harder than ever. His employees had never failed him before—until now. He had been the only one holding it together. Breaking even was a rare victory in today's market and trying just wasn't worth it anymore. He gazed out the window to the city. Maybe he ought to quit and get away from all this; it was obviously too much stress for him. He could just escape from it all and start over.

That night, Eugene made a phone call to one of the best architects New York. He decided he was going to build a new house, secluded far up in the mountains, where he could avoid the poverty that polluted this city. And he would sell his firm, escaping from the dreadful responsibility of managing such a train wreck.

At first, Eugene was planning something small, just a small estate, perhaps only five thousand square feet or so. But when the architect quoted a price of only $25,000, Eugene laughed heartily. That wasn't even a fraction of his wealth. Eugene told the architect to make the house as big and grand as he could in the same remote area; a place that would provide solitude away from the pestilence of humanity that scourged the outside world but still had all the luxuries of it.

Only a week later, Eugene met the architect in his office. During the car ride over, he'd hardly been able to contain himself, his imagination let loose with wild ideas of what his new home might be—massive corridors with junctions to others within just a few steps from each other; a ballroom with a vaulted ceiling so high it got lost out of sight into the heavens; towering spires above deep catacombs that were too long and too numerous to chart. His mind had circulated through these wishful ideas until he'd arrived at the architect's office. And as the architect unrolled a huge piece of parchment paper, Eugene watched as his dreams died in an instant, his limitless imagination stamped out by the limits of reality. "It's too small!" Eugene responded despondently. "Where are my guests supposed to stay?"

"Don't worry, Mr. Motter. There are plenty of rooms," the architect assured him.

"No ... No ... I don't think so." Eugene looked at the blueprints blankly. His hand rested under his chin as he studied the page, until he saw a pencil lying where it had been tossed on the other end of the desk. He grabbed it with a confident smirk on his face and drew two crude rectangles extending off the precisely drawn blueprint model. The architect looked insulted as he drew, nearly ripping the pencil out of Eugene's hand.

"There! Like that! Do that!" Eugene demanded, staring haughtily at the mortified architect.

"Do what?!" the architect almost yelled, unable to contain his anger at the destruction of what he'd been working on over the past week.

"See these are extensions for the home, wings." Eugene pointed to the two misshaped rectangles expanding off the home.

"You don't understand," the architect protested. "There isn't enough room for that!"

"I don't care," Eugene snarled. "Make room. Find a new location. Make it happen! I don't pay you to fail me!"

The architect stood in silence outraged by his client's difficulty, but he took a closer look at the damaged blueprint after Eugene had left the office. The architect applied practicality to the two outlandish wings Eugene had drawn and started a new map with the project title "North Haven" scrawled in the top right corner.

CHAPTER 3

North Haven

A bright, new morning light had crossed the horizon, caressing the freshly tiled roof that covered the new estate of North Haven. After two years of construction and constant impatience from the buyer, the palace that teased the envious eyes of humanity had come to life. Workers and inspectors scrambled in and out of the building adding final touches until the fine-tuned motor of a four and a half-litre Bentley rumbled up the mountain, warning of the forthcoming deadline. The Bentley pulled up in the unfinished, gravel driveway, where a chief inspector greeted Eugene and was quickly dismissed with the rest of his workers to evacuate the site.

Eugene Motter had brought only his family—the one thing he cared about most—to his new life. Everything else could be replaced. The four who followed stepped out of the car, Eugene's wife, Pearl Motter, a loving mother of three; his two boys, Robert and Jack; and his oldest, Jessica.

Through the months of constantly prodding the work crew, Eugene had managed to shorten the deadline by three months, and when news had come that the estate was nearly finished, Eugene had hastily assembled the family, interrupting whatever each was doing to show them the surprise he had hidden from them for years. Now they stood in awe at the side entrance of the palace, under the massive shadow cast down upon them by the home's colossal stature. Eugene turned around to face his family, his arms wide in the air as if he was holding the home on his shoulders.

"What do you think?" Eugene burst out as he looked at his family's reaction. "Of our new home," he added.

"Our new home?" Pearl questioned because two hours ago they had just been at their home. "But we already have a home."

"Well, now we have a new one!" Eugene added excitedly.

"But what about..." Pearl began.

"Pearl, don't worry about that; this is our new one. We have a fresh start now!" Eugene said with a grin that could only barely explain his excitement.

Pearl bit her lip as she took in the unforeseen life change and tried to share her husband's happiness with a forced smile. Eugene would do something like this.

"Don't you love it?"

"Of course!" she bellowed out. "I'm just a little surprised is all."

"I knew you would!" Eugene said smiling, his eyes brightened with their approval. As Pearl looked into her husband's eyes, she couldn't help but be reminded of how much she loved him, and she convinced herself that her husband's happiness was all that really mattered.

Eugene led his family inside, into a small foyer with walkways encircling above them and railed by marble banisters. Simple-shaped tiles lay in a pattern across the foyer floor, mirroring and complementing each other in a complex, spiraling design. The small size of the foyer appeared disproportionate to the outside of the home. The entrance was grand, but it did not seem grand enough for such a palace.

"We live here now, Dad?" asked eight-year-old Robert, his head pivoting, unable to see the full scope of the majesty of the home in a single frame of reference.

"Yes," his father replied, lying his hand over his son's shoulder.

"I thought we lived back in New York City?" Robert asked.

"Well we live here now," Eugene said. "Our own little slice of heaven away from all that humdrum."

"What about all my friends though?" Robert whimpered.

"Well ..." His father hesitated. "I guess you'll just have to find something else to do," he finished apathetically. "Come on; let me give you the grand tour." Eugene took off in one direction with Pearl trailing not far behind, herding Robert with one arm and holding Jack close to her with the other. Jessica lagged along still looking around.

* * *

Jordan's eyes burst wide open; she awoke with an abrupt sense of urgency. She rubbed her eyes and sat up from the comfortable sleeping bag to check the time. It was 11:17 p.m. She shook her head out of annoyance and confusion and lay back until she realized the door was wide open now, welcoming her into the unsettling black mouth of the hall.

"I thought I closed that," she mumbled as she tried to close her eyes. She couldn't help but turn away from the hallway's open invitation, her mind too focused on lost sleep to care about the open door. She tried again to close her tired eyes before realizing that they didn't want to stay shut, and after a few minutes of tossing and turning, she turned back to the open door. *Maybe I can walk this off.*

She crawled out of her sleeping bag and walked into the gaping throat, disappearing into the darkness. Overwhelming blackness demeaned the careful placement of each step as she attempted to make her way through the dark. By chance alone, she found her way to the foyer. The gibbous moon shined through the upper foyer windows that encompassed the second floor above her. With the minimal amount of light the moon offered, Jordan walked in a more composed fashion down the steps of the staircase, her feet cringing with every step across the cold marble floor, until she had centered herself in the room.

* * *

"Now this is only the back entrance; the front entrance doesn't have a road leading up to it yet, but it's in the works. It will be paved," Eugene reassured his family as he led them through the side foyer. "We're in the west wing right now, the guest wing."

"How big is this place?" Pearl asked, taken aback by the notion that it was even bigger than what they had seen already.

"Darling, just wait and see," Eugene said, as if he was addressing a bigger, more important crowd. "The guest wing features dozens of rooms to give our future guests the treatment they deserve, as well as servants' quarters so that future guests are not spared from any luxury."

Eugene led his family through a massive hallway. The group was flanked by the whitest of walls, brightened even more by the outstanding red sheen superimposed onto them by the priceless rosewood that stretched along the hall's floor. A magnificent, master-crafted, vaulted ceiling paralleled the floor, continuing until the two ran off into the distant horizon. Decorative arches ordained the ceiling above, placed where no eyes would bother to look.

To Pearl, it was all so overwhelming. The house was truly spectacular and extraordinary, but it wasn't a home. No, this was a boundless, ornate labyrinth that would only divide a family. A family could live in this place and not see each other for days. As she stood now admiring just a hallway, she had never felt so withdrawn from her family, for here, the vastness of this place diluted any feeling of unity between them.

"Whoa!" Jack shouted as he ran down the hallway. His outline grew smaller and smaller the farther he ventured as the home's greatness took him away.

"Jack, wait! You'll get lost!" shouted Pearl.

Eugene just laughed. "Let him be, Pearl. He likes the place too, see!" Eugene remarked. "Let's go try and catch up with him," he suggested, urging the rest of the family with a wave of his hand.

* * *

Jordan wasn't far behind the long-forgotten tour. She looked down the vast hallway and what had once been great was now eroded and dulled down to nothing but a littered passage. She began to check the doors in the hall. They were all locked. The imprint where numbers once had hung stained the tops of doors, and only a few doors were fortunate enough to be spared maybe one rusted number.

With nowhere to go but forward, Jordan continued down the hall carefully placing each step with careful consideration in the darkness. She cursed herself the whole way for not turning back for a flash light. Silhouettes of fallacious shadows skulked and lingered just beyond discernible sight. An occasional unsolicited tap or creak would interrupt the silence inclining her to believe that she was not alone. She was trapped in between the hallway walls with whatever else might have been with her. This was a bad idea, she thought as she tried to wade through the darkness. *I should just go back to bed.*

She didn't; undeterred by the night, she continued to stumble though the unwelcoming blackness.

*   *   *

Eugene led his wife and children down the hall. Doors lined most of the hall's right side, and ignoring her husband's disinterest, Pearl stopped to peak into one of the many doors, only to be met by a disapproving glare from over her husband's shoulder. She bit her lip in bitter compliance and continued to follow her husband.

Eugene had been blindly leading them in circles around the home as he tried to figure which way was the right one in his own home. One random turn after another led them out to a high, vaulted hallway that faced the true front of the home.

"This is what I was looking for! The main hall," Eugene explained.

The main hall was a massive opening that spanned across the entire facing of the house. Marble arches rose above and beyond their heads, vaulting the sky above them. Paned windows as tall as the hall they decorated lined the entire front facing, allowing the morning sun to cast the sharp outline of the window panes across the refulgent marble. Small chandeliers hung unlit, spaced evenly and carefully over the length of the hall and centering toward one grand one in the center of the main Foyer. Eugene had stood, motionless in his steps, smiling; demonstrating his pride for his new home.

"Jessica, can you go find your brother before he gets so lost we can't find him? And take Robert with you so maybe I can have a talk with your father," Pearl whispered, now that her disillusioned husband was distracted. Jessica instinctively nodded to her mother and left.

Eugene didn't even bother to notice the side conversation, and after taking in all the greatness of this place, he continued down the hall.

* * *

Wandering in the dark led Jordan to an intersection in the hall, with both passageways leading in questionable directions. She looked with uncertainty to her right; that hall led to a completely blackened corridor. Glancing back to the hall straight ahead of her, she saw that windows along it allowed the outside light to partially light the way. The choice seemed obvious. But after two uneasy footsteps forward, she heard a shuffling like the sound of other footsteps and the wood floor of the hall to her right creaked. She stopped and shook her head as she listened to the other footsteps trail off down the right hall. Knowing she couldn't ignore the idea that someone else might be here, she turned to her right and set off down the hall, hoping to find the other intruder.

Jordan chased the footsteps to the end of the hall, which led into a large, gusting draft from the end of the hall and out into a ray of moonlight that shined down from a tall window. The footsteps had stopped, and after realizing she had stepped past the hall and into a different one, Jordan turned to look down the expansive maw of the main hall. It was from there that Jordan finally saw the full size of this palace she was intruding in. A grand hall connected and stretched past the wing that she stayed in and led far away to what looked like another wing at the opposite end of the hall.

* * *

Jack wandered through the random path of doors that only ever opened to even more paths. Jack's eyes and head were roamed incessantly as he tried to explore every corner of the home. He found his way to what looked like another pointless, little hall. Jack had been wandering for more than ten minutes and still couldn't find any end to their new home. It was then that he realized that the wall to his right was ruffled and folded in like a cloth. He pulled back the veil to be surprised by an audience of bright red, empty chairs arranged in neat, compact columns all watching him as he walked onto the center stage. An imagined spotlight was now on him, and a pressure to perform forced him to improvise. He adjusted his imaginary top hat and addressed the audience.

"For my next trick"—he paused dramatically; his voice echoed and filled every seat of the auditorium full of suspense—"a dozen doves will fly out of my hat." He ripped his hat off in a spectacular fashion as a dozen doves of a child's imagination flew away in a single direction in the room.

Jessica stood nonchalantly in the entrance to the auditorium watching a child do nothing but believing he did everything. As he stood there marveling in the triumph of his own imagination, an unanticipated "boo" pulled him from the limitless horizons of his mind back down to the inescapable gravity of reality. He looked around the auditorium, both startled and annoyed, to try and find the perpetrator. His sister stood in the main entrance to the doorway leaning carelessly on its frame with a harmless, playful smile written across her face.

"Awww, Jessica, why do you always have to ruin my fun?" Jack said as he leaped from the stage, knowing exactly why his sister was there.

"Because you know not to run off and you always do it." she answered.

Jack now walked past her, and she trailed him, keeping an authoritative but loving hand on his shoulder.

Eugene and Pearl had continued down the main hall toward the main foyer. Inside the grand entrance, a domineering ceiling arched overhead with beautiful, engraved marble boasting the same spiraling designs found throughout the home. Two grand staircases unfurled themselves across the foyer floor, mirroring one another. Their bases nearly came together in the center but instead were interrupted by a door in between them. A second-story balcony hung aloof from above but remained mostly out of sight from the limited vista of the foyer. All of this came together to make a perfect introduction to their palace of excess.

By now, it had all stopped surprising Pearl. Nothing was underdone, and no expense had been spared to make this place a pinnacle of luxury, when all it really was was a landmark of excess and vanity—unnecessary beauty and glory that would never be wholly appreciated by just one man or one family.

"Here we are! This is the best part!" Eugene exclaimed with such excitement that it bordered a yell. "The main wing; this will be where our rooms are, as well as the ballroom and its accessory rooms." He led his wife through the opening betwixt the two curling staircases to a massive ballroom that opened up above to encompass windows similar to those in the main hall. Daylight glared through the western side beaming down on the eastern wall and imposing a bright silhouette of the window panes above. Squared away at the far end of the elongated room was an elevated platform a few feet high—just high enough that people could gather to see future bands play or for a speaker to address a group of business clients. But for now, it was just an empty stage. Decorative bordering swathed the room's arches and edges, elegant enough to keep up with the pomp of the rest of the home but too subtle to make an overall impression when up against the void of the colossal room. Eugene walked toward the center, losing himself in the grandness.

"What are we going to do with place?" Pearl finally let out the unbearable question.

Eugene turned around to face his wife. Somehow, though he stood in the same room as her, he felt so far away. "What do you mean? What can't we do with a place like this!" he quipped as he gave a hearty laugh.

Pearl, almost anticipating his reply, looked at the ground. Disheartened, she shook her head.

"I thought you liked it. I did it for us, you know?" Eugene responded with the tact of a four-year-old.

"No it's nice, but isn't it a little much?" Pearl asked.

"Oh don't be ridiculous!" Eugene smiled, ignoring his wife's concern. "I bought only the best for the family, and I wouldn't have done it any other way!"

Pearl smiled at her husband's effort. Although he may have never been the most affectionate father, he always showed his love in indirect and misinterpreted ways. "You know what?" Pearl interjected. "I love it! It was just kind of overwhelming at first."

Eugene gave her a gleaming, white smile as he laughed. "I knew you'd come around!" he said excitedly. "You always do."

He strayed away from the center of the room and back toward his wife, grabbing her by the hand and linking himself to her by the hip.

Swaying with him, Pearl was reminded of why she loved this man. As insensitive as he may be, he always tried.

As they slowly waltzed around the ballroom to the unperceivable sway of a silent minuet that guided each step, the two locked gazes, expressing a wordless desire and affection for one another.

"I still remember the day I swept you away," he whispered into her ear as the two made a graceful synchronized march across the marble floor.

"You asked for a dance and never let me go," she replied coyly.

"Oh please, you never let me go," he said. "Not to mention that New Jersey boy you came with didn't know a thing about dancing."

"It's true. He stepped on my foot at least a dozen times that night."

Eugene laughed at the remark, taking pride in that small triumph that had eventuated in a lifetime of fulfillment.

*   *   *

Jordan, now for the first time, saw the true entrance of the home. The main foyer opened wide to its spanning marble floors. Here, dimly lit by the fading moonlight, was the most well preserved room in the entire home. Where rust and rot had made their infectious march throughout the home, this room had been spared. Jordan took a gander at the imposing entrance, her eyes and feet wandering carelessly around the room until an inviting, open door caught her attention. Between the two staircases, a set of doors had been left completely open, as if a lure for wandering eyes. Jordan ceased her wandering and headed to the doors.

The ancient ballroom where, unknown to her, Eugene had danced with his wife eighty years earlier was now crumbling. The tall, stone walls had cracked under the unbearable weight of time. The floor was covered in the dust of age and ruin. Arches expanded across the walls of the ballroom, opening to windows. All that was left in the room was a curious, decrepit grand piano sitting in the center of the far-off stage. Leaning on a broken leg, the marred piano strayed just beyond the reach of the moonlit windows. Jordan wandered toward the grand piano over the stone tiles that spiraled across the floor in different shades of marble integrating into a pattern across the ballroom floor.

She jumped up on the stage and looking down at its jagged, craggy keys; it resembled a once beautiful white set of teeth now deranged into an uneven mess and yellowed by age. Jordan tried one of the keys; the response was a strained, flat D. She pressed down on a C and got no response at all. A little disappointed, she turned back to the prodigious ballroom. She looked up to see shadows mingling in the far-off corners, careful not to be exposed to light or visibility—two unmistakable figures of men facing each other as if casually chatting.

"Hello?" Jordan asked. No response came from the unfazed shadows.

She stepped off the stage and began to go after the still shadows. As she drew closer, the clouding veil of her imagination dissipated, revealing the reality that there was nothing there but the stonework of the walls. She shook her head at her naive actions and knew she should probably just go back to bed and explore more in the daylight, or at least with a flashlight. She exited the ballroom, closing its two grand doors and leaving the limping piano and the shadows to their seclusion.

*   *   *

Pearl and Eugene exited the ballroom now, looking for their children. "So do you like it?" Eugene eagerly asked, reaffirming his excitement and chasing out doubt.

"Of course, but I think it needs furniture," she added cleverly.

"That's tomorrow!" Eugene declared with excitement. "Just wait till you see what I bought!" They crossed over into the hall and looked back as he carefully closed the door behind him, so as not to disturb the absent guests in the ballroom.

CHAPTER 4

North Haven

Three loud, urgent taps on the lone window woke Jordan from a nearly sleepless night. Dumbfounded by the tapping, she dragged herself out of the warmth of the cozy sleeping bag to the frigid morning air to look out the window to another gray day. She saw the day as alive as it would ever be but no sign from the unknown knocker. She tapped the window, mimicking the unwelcome wake-up call. Entertaining the idea that someone else might be here only made her feel more unwelcome, and given the continued string of bizarre incidents, she felt her stay may need to be ended sooner than later.

She lay back in her sleeping bag, intending to keep warm from the nipping cold morning air and go back to sleep. But her busy mind had other intentions. Closed eyes did nothing but peel right back open to stare at the blank ceiling. Conceding to the fact that she was wide awake anyway, she convinced herself it was time to start the day despite her lack of sleep. Forcing herself to brave the frigid morning, she fought off the cozy folds of the sleeping bag with a heavy sigh and forced herself out.

After the unsettling start to her day, Jordan grabbed a blank notebook in which she had planned to record her stay and started by following her unsighted steps from the night before. After last night's midnight exploration, she had figured out that maybe she had underestimated the true size of this place.

She walked out the door to a less menacing world than the one she'd left behind the night before. The imposing hallways from last night that had seemed to hide menacing phantoms around each corner in the obscurity of darkness now shriveled under the light of a new day and their size. Jordan's pencil began to draw out parallel lines as she followed the walls on each side of the corridor, mapping the contours that shaped the home. Despite the fact that most of the corridors paralleled each other and were relatively straight, her map worked out to be an uneven, jagged mess of lines.

It wasn't as if it had mattered anyway. Most of what the house had to offer was behind locked doors. The rooms behind the few doors that did open for Jordan looked as if they had been ransacked in the past, with nothing left behind save for dust marks on the floors outlining where furniture was and where paintings had formerly hung.

Most of the accessible rooms on the west side were uniformly sized, each featuring a similar bathroom and room design. The high volume of rooms and their conforming layout suggested something like a hotel. But the idea of a hotel out in the middle of the woods sounded ludicrous.

Following an aimless path weaving in and out of each corridor, Jordan surveyed the place and mapped it by memory. With the west half seemingly covered, it only felt right to move on to the other parts of the home. She traveled along the large hallway she had traversed the night before. Darkness had obscured strewn debris piled by past gales into the corners and along the edges of the grand hall.

Jordan stopped intermittently on her path down the expansive hall, attempting to hear something that followed in between her firm footsteps on the cold, stone floor. But in each pause, she was met only by the nulling silence that had passively resonated here since whatever past voice had previously dared break it. Mapping it all out made her image of this place more wholesome, despite it not really answering the most lingering question of who had lived here.

To her undue surprise, the doors to the ballroom, which she'd closed the night before were still closed. She approached the two doors cautiously, still a little incredulous as to their unaltered state, and opened them carefully. A rusty-sounding creak from the door allowed her passage into the massive ballroom. The limping piano remained on watch alone, continuing its eternal vigil as it stood above the ballroom's main floor but ready to collapse under the weight of a finger. Jordan crossed the ballroom and climbed up on the stage, joining the grand old piano for a better vantage point. She glanced around the walls, she noticed two sets of handwritten pages resting side by side on the piano stand that had escaped her the night before. Edges curled, stained, and forgotten, the stack on the right was drafted sheet music, every written note squared away. It was slightly more stained and aged than the stack on the left; the pages in this stack had been crumpled and the notes written on them were scribbled over and crossed out, hiding assumed fallacies.

Jordan could barely read sheet music; she knew only notes and most rhythmic symbols. But even she could recognize that what was finished was just a simple melody. Her inexperience forced her to count the lines to translate the notes, and she played them slowly, her hand creeping along the keys without rhythm. She hit a dead key just into the third measure and stopped herself. She grabbed both the readable and scribbled pile of papers and tucked them behind her notes before taking off for the door.

She walked into the main foyer and faced the two massive hallways that led away from it, each a debris-strewn corridor imposing endless choices on where to go next. Jordan looked down both expanses of the hall before turning around to look up at the elusive upstairs, its loft dimly lit and its corridors receding into the darker parts of the home. Jordan reevaluated her options, poking her head past the wall to see the overwhelming expanse of the east wing and then staring back at the unpleasant, ominous darkness of the upper main wing. Dissatisfied with both choices, she thought up a third one and turned her back to what looked like the actual front door. Figuring that, when she'd started, she'd never gotten a good look around the home's exterior, she decided to take a quick tour around the grounds, and then afterward, she'd work her way to the east side or the upper main level.

The two grand doors of the main foyer opened up to a panoramic vista of the entire front lawn. The lawn was a wild, overgrown stretch of oak trees aligned in a linear pattern between columns of grass underneath weeds. The front lawn was probably larger than five acres in total, stretching from the the house to the distant stone walls. Cobblestone paths spewed out of the base of the entrance and divided and split the lawn into misshaped polygons with thick, gray outlines defining their edges. Jordan stepped down the purposely monumental set of stairs that led up to the entrance to the grand palace and set off on the path that led along the left side of the home.

Its course curved along the side lawn, which was expectedly unimpressive. The enclosing stone wall was placed only thirty feet away from the house, stopping any sort of sprawling view. The path continued parallel to the wall before curving off to the back end of the home.

From the edge of the south lawn outlined by the stone walls, the house was partially hidden behind the curvature of the hill and the loose column of oak trees that mirrored the direction of the path. The stone walkway Jordan had followed curved and toured around the edge of the property before ending at its final stop: the trail to the main gate. For the first time, Jordan finally saw the true eclipsing size of the home. as it dominated the narrow horizon. Built on the highest hill of the clearing, it claimed its territory between the trees. The home's front was decorated with a rising colonnade. Windows peered from the spaces between the columns, which rose to hold up the large portico laureling the home with chiseled, decorative wreaths and curving spirals. The house stood atop the hill like a fainting piece of time, decrepit and old. Its stone, once brightly colored, had faded into a somber gray that only whispered of its former glory. Its face, as if hammered and scored by elusive chisels, once a covenant of luxury and grandeur for the many, now remained a scar alone in the woods.

Jordan leaned on a stone wall that separated the cobblestone road she was now on from the overgrown lawn and took a moment to watch as the house passively crumbled away. What a tragedy. For something that had probably been so mighty and admired to be abandoned without regard. Knowing that someone had willingly walked away from something so majestic and refined was hard to understand. Thousands of meticulous hours of labor, the memories of someone's family, the pride of someone's legacy had been left to rot with no concern.

She stopped herself from dwelling. A small gatehouse behind her stopped the road from going any farther, and Jordan figured that was where the main road led. She couldn't really be sure, but the archaic iron gate securing the estate seemed to have been irresponsibly left ajar. She walked over to investigate, only to find that the gate was indeed open and that it led to nowhere. An open clearing was all that remained outside the gate before the surrounding forest.

Dark, ominous clouds had begun to churn in the sky; violet blue billows hinted of rain. She closed the gate behind her before following the trail up to the estate.

As she entered the home through its grand front double doors, the ghostly silhouette of the grand piano that sat center stage between the two wide open doors leading to the ballroom welcomed her. She was pretty sure she'd closed those doors. Trying to ignore her childish imagination, she fled upstairs, avoiding its enigmatic beckoning.

The stairs of the main foyer brought her to a loft that peered over the ballroom and was connected on both sides by halls that reached out east and west to their corresponding wings. She followed the westward hall and then abruptly stopped, realizing she'd passed an unremarkable, wooden door. Predicting it to be locked, she gave the doorknob a light turn, only for it to give way under her minimal pressure. She stopped with an eager grin to look inside and all the expected things one would find in a bedroom were still there—a bed, a dresser, a night stand, an old radio—a miraculous sign that someone had once lived here.

Jordan scrambled into the room only to ransack it. Nothing was safe as she started to rummage through everything that could hide a secret. Whatever might have been resting in that home wasn't anymore as the drawers of the dresser grinded in protest as Jordan opened each one. Nothing but molded clothes had been left in the dresser and closet. She blew off the dust from on top of the radio as she scrambled around the room looking. Jordan, desperate for a clue, widened her search, she peeked under the bed in hopes of finding whatever it was she was looking for An old wooden box was hidden behind one of the legs of the bed.

She violently pulled her discovery out to see what it hid. Prying open the wooden box's ornate lid, she found a stack of paper, letters—each started with the opening, "Dear Robert."

CHAPTER 5

The Stranger at the Gala

Robert found himself engulfed in the promenade of people that regularly came to North Haven. The modern day nobles that ruled the Western world were all invited to his father's weekly balls. The likes of statesmen to businessmen were welcome to bring their families and spend an evening "the way the Motters do it" as his father always put it. Here, the nobility of the world would gather like speckles of dust across the ballroom floor to indulge in a night of drinking, dancing, and entertainment. Robert, being one of the unremarkable speckles among the estates, never could find a place at his dad's parties.

"They're friends of the family," his father always answered whenever Robert asked who all these people were. They certainly weren't his friends, and Robert was pretty sure they weren't his father's either. His father was always in it for things other than friendship. Other people's happiness wasn't ever apart of his agenda; being noticed was really what he was after. Conversations that may have only referenced his name in passing warranted his attention and approval. His father was only happy when everyone in the room was happy with him.

Robert shared the same need for self-worth as his father. Hiding only admitted a self-defeat that he didn't want to live with and he didn't want to be seen alone so he would wander through the crowds pretending to be someone. He never felt socially inclined or interested in talking with or meeting any of these people, so he avoided doing so when he could. He just couldn't find anything meaningful to say to any of them. At times, he couldn't escape being randomly grabbed by his mother or father to be shown off to their friends. During these moments, all Robert could manage was an awkward "Hello" before slinking off into an invented social life of his.

As he maneuvered through the crowds of people to retreat to a nearby hall, a voice from behind him sung out, "Hey, you, wait!"

Robert stopped for a moment before realizing the girl who'd called out wasn't looking for him. But a snag on his suit stopped him from continuing on.

"Are you going to stop and introduce yourself?" The very same voice that had been calling for someone else was now being directed at Robert.

Robert looked behind him to see a gorgeous, young brunette girl. She was shorter than Robert but made up for the difference with her arms placed at her hips outlining her outrage. "Hey, I'm Sierra!" she said with a slight nod of her head.

"Hi ..." Robert, caught off guard by this girl's outspokenness, replied the best he could.

"Did you forget your name?" she asked with a laugh.

"No! My name is Robert," he replied, completely baffled now.

"Well, it's a pleasure to meet you, Robert!" she said after shaking his hand "Say, Robert, what are you doing?" she asked, sounding more like she was confirming a hunch rather than genuinely curious.

"I'm ... I'm ... going to the dining room to get some food." he lied.

"Really. Looks like you've been going to the dining room over and over again for the past hour," she said.

"Maybe," he admitted. "But I have to go!" he said, wiggling his way into the crowd.

"Wait! Where are you going?" Robert heard her yell out from behind as he made his way through the crowd. He slipped out the door and continued walking at a brisk pace down the hall, relieved he'd gotten away. That encounter couldn't have been any more humiliating. He made his way to the foyer and began up the stairs to escape at least this party, until a voice echoed down the hall.

"Hey, wait! Come back!"

It was her again. Robert let out a groan as he froze in his steps. Stopping didn't feel like a good idea, but Robert respected her effort. She stood at the base of the stairs looking up at him as he teetered on the decision of running or maybe just staying. He turned to toward the girl, taken by a cowardly look of shame and helplessness. "I'm sorry, Sierra. I don't think I can help you with what you need," he replied timidly. He stared at the ground below her, trying to avoid eye contact.

"Why not?"

"I'm just not really the best person to have a conversation with. What do you want anyway?"

"I don't know ... I guess I just wanted to get to know you," she said, each word hesitating to follow the last.

With a sigh of humiliation, he smirked to himself. He stepped down from his high, judgmental step in humility to meet this person who'd made such an effort to meet him. "What did you want to know?" Robert mumbled shyly.

"I don't know, Robert. Tell me about yourself," she said.

"Well, I'm Robert Motter, and I live here," he began.

Sierra looked at him with annoyance and let out a sigh, indicating she was tired from her tedious effort. "Maybe I should start," she said. "I'm Sierra Rhodes, daughter of Daniel Rhodes. He's a friend of your father's, I guess. I'm fifteen years old and live in New York City. I like horseback riding, dancing, and gossip!" she added, hyping the last part a little too much.

Robert wanted to slap his head in shame, coming to the simple conclusion that she *was* a girl.

"See! Nothing too complicated!"

"Well, I'm Robert Motter. My dad is Eugene Motter, and my mother is Pearl. I guess for fun I mostly just play the piano and read," he said cautiously.

"I see," Sierra drawled out. "Are you good at playing the piano?"

"Of course!" Robert boasted, outraged by such a question. His head perked up out of his timid and shrunken composure.

She smiled back, and he sulked, lowering his head after realizing that he'd gotten a little too excited.

"Well, are you going to play for me?" she asked eagerly.

Robert thought about it. *She is really nice ... and pretty.* But he had never played for anyone, and if he could barely talk to her, how well would he fair playing for her? "Well I can't right now. The piano's in the ballroom," he said finally.

"Are you telling me there is only one piano in this giant mansion?" she blurted incredulously.

"Maybe ..." Robert continued vaguely.

Hiding in his lie didn't seem to work, as she grabbed his hand with a disbelieving look but a convincing smile and cheered out the most dreaded words Robert could have imagine. "C'mon; let's go find a piano."

Robert couldn't resist any longer, and he gladly let Sierra drag him away.

Sierra led Robert down the main hall of the west wing. She had him by his hand as he reluctantly but compliantly followed her, secretly enjoying it.

"Wow this place is big!" She said in amazement. She turned to look at Robert, who looked unfazed by the wonder of the design he had known his whole life.

As she wandered blindly, leading him through the dark hallways, he followed along, knowing exactly where they were going. Once they'd left behind the glowing ballroom and the adjoining main foyer, the light had faded, and they'd worked their way into the forgotten dark edges of the home, where the previously unseen moonlight now amended the darkness of the night. As the distant sounds of the mingling guests and the live music dissipated into the labyrinth of halls, all that could be heard were the soft pairs of footsteps advancing one after the other and echoing into the distance and far beyond, eluding time's corrosive sway—the overture to a new prospect to Roberts's life.

A large double-door entranceway interrupted the long, stone wall along the main hall. "What's in here?" Sierra asked, curiously peeking through the door. The moment the door opened an astounded look took over her face. The welcoming expanse of the auditorium waited on the other side of the door. Oddly enough, someone had left all the lights on, probably to display the room to whoever might wander in. Robert walked past her with a vain smile that showed more hauteur than genuine happiness.

"I guess my dad must've left the lights on," Robert noted.

"Wow! This place is amazing. Why does your family have a theater this big?" Sierra asked as she looked around.

"Because we can," he explained "or at least that's what my dad says. He always brags about how he could bring the shows to us," Robert boasted, trying not to be smug. But he felt a lot of pride in owning her fascination.

She began to take those first few lost steps of amazement, and then she turned around with a look on her face that foretold the epiphany she'd just had. "There has to be a piano in here!" she clamored.

Robert, playing along with her pointless search, rolled his eyes as he followed, aware of the fact that the only other piano was in the opposite wing. She proceeded to check every corner of the stage, looking for the legendary second piano but found nothing. Meanwhile, Robert only deviously smiled to himself as she looked away but suddenly became just as befuddled when she glared at him with a questioning look.

After every corner had been scoured with no piano in sight, their search took a turn in an odd direction—the unpolished underside of North Haven. Sierra led her search into the service corridors that filled the space in between the walls. A door to the east wing's boiler rooms were the first to be checked. Robert wondered how long he could keep up the act, as the second piano was in the opposite wing. Even he had only been in the service corridors a few times, as the only thing down here was storage for servants and house utilities.

"Wait! What's this?" she said as she pulled out, to Robert's surprise, an old spinet piano hiding behind some shelving.

"I ... I don't know," Robert stuttered, wondering where in the it had come from.

"It's a piano, stupid. You know, the one I was talking about."

"I know, but ..." Robert continued, realizing he might have to play for her after all.

"But nothin'. Now let's see how good you *really* are," she said, grabing a nearby crate a patting the top of it in a gesture suggesting he take a seat.

He couldn't say no by this point. He hesitantly took a seat in front of the piano and flipped open the cover. Ten years of experiences didn't feel like enough preparation to play in front of her. His start was slow and stalled as his fingers struggled to find the right key but as he went through the motions, muscle memory guided him through the rest. While his right hand scaled through the keys his left hammered down the chords, he mezzo forted a seamless performance of *Moonlight Sonata*. Robert, engaged in his music, distracted himself by staring emptily at the vacant music stand. Note for note, the playing came naturally. But the intensity with which he played never ended, and as much as he would have liked to be cocky, he dared not misplay for fear of tarnishing some invaluable reputation he'd apparently established with her. He wanted to look back and see her face.

After the lifetime that passed in only fifteen long minutes and with the final, most intense part of the piece, Robert carried the end of the movement with such flair that he was sure astound her. He took a moment to stretch his fingers and looked back to see her reaction.

"You're pretty good," she said with only a smile.

"You mean pretty and good?" Robert retorted and immediately shrunk back in his posture, realizing he let his ego slip.

"Nope! Just pretty good! If you were better than that, you wouldn't be so nervous about playing to me." She mocked him. "But, you are pretty though." A moment of silence followed as Robert tried to hide his blush from her allowing the faded music from the ballroom to leak through the walls. A distinguishable upbeat minuet was playing from the party downstairs.

A large booming of instruments shook the stillness of the boiler room as the minuet proceeded into its major movement. Robert, faced with an uncomfortable silence between them, listened to the dissociated music for a moment until a bold idea popped into his head. He stood up from the piano and turned around towards Sierra and gently grabbed her by the hand with a slight bow. "May I have this dance?" he asked, looking up into her eyes. He felt so cliché but charming, as with a delighted smile and surprised eyes, Sierra just couldn't say no.

"Of course."

Robert embraced her at the hip and held her by the hand, slowly leading her across the room and gliding to the dampened rhythm of the far-off dance. As they swayed under the unappreciated hanging light bulb, Robert's gaze was lost in hers, and he returned a mutual smile of appreciation.

"You were fantastic, by the way," Sierra interjected midway through the dance.

"Fantastic at what?" he asked, confused by the digression.

"At playing," she continued.

"Better than pretty good?" Robert asked brazenly.

"Maybe just a little," she replied as she rested her head on his shoulder.

They danced for a few moments longer as the music died down to its subtle end. For the last song of the night, Robert held Sierra just a little longer before saying good-bye.

"Maybe I'll see you at the next party," she said, sounding hopeful.

"Maybe," he replied somewhat dubiously.

"Well if the party is over, my parents are probably looking for me. I've got to go," she said, breaking away from Robert's shoulder to give him the mournful look of good-bye. "I had a good time, though."

"Not even pretty good?" he said, smiling, quite proud of his scintillating remark.

"It was fantastic! But I have to go. I'll see you next time," she said with a delightful wave of her fingers as she walked out the door.

"Bye," Robert said, a little lost for words as he sadly raised his hand to wave good-bye.

As she disappeared out the door and the echo of her footsteps receded into the hallway, Robert took a seat on a nearby chair, his mind wrapped around all that happened during the night. He liked Sierra, but a deep sense of mistrust in reality forced him to be wary and cynical about all that had taken place. He stopped himself from entirely killing the mood. It had been a fun night for once and he should treat it as such.

CHAPTER 6

Clandestine Getaways

Saturday afternoons and sometimes Fridays passed along with a mixture of excitement and nervousness, as Robert tensely waited for the week to culminate into his only chance to see Sierra. The past few weeks had followed in the same manner; the patient anxious waiting that was always proven to be a worth it. He had begun to really like her and, along with that, he dreaded the time in between the weekends during which he had to wait to see her.

On these Saturday afternoons, North Haven followed along with Robert as it prepared for the same rapturous excitement and stress in anticipation for the party. Servants adorned the halls with streamers and flyers, following the arbitrary theme for the night, while cooks attempted to prepare the finest meals for the dozens who'd be attending. Maids prepared rooms and removed any suspicion of uncleanliness from the imposing corridors that already swallowed the presence of any speck of dust. It was this harmonious rhythm of work of the forgettable servants that made North Haven manageable.

During the summer, North Haven offered work to over twenty servants; five groundskeepers nurtured the spanning gardens of the estate, eight maids cleaned the guests rooms and provided the necessary luxuries for them, four more wandered the entire length of the home cleaning its neglected rooms and halls, three cooks prepared meals for the family and their usual guests, one repair man aimlessly wandered the maintenance halls with nothing to do, and two other servants did assorted tasks of odds and ends, like getting the mail, but mostly supervised the other servants. In the winter, this number dropped to a mere ten, with fewer guests and frozen gardens; the need for servants fluctuated with the seasons. Each brought along his or her own family. Spouses were typically also employed for the well-being of North Haven, and the servants' children were left cramped within the home's servants' quarters. In the peak of summer, North Haven had over forty people at a time living within its walls, only four of whom were Motters.

Robert watched under the blinding glare of the tall glass windows of the main hall as servants scurried by. He had taken to quietly sitting in the main hall on these tedious afternoons to mentally prepare himself for later that night, rehearsing in his head what he might say and figuring how coy he might just be.

A whisper carried on from down the hall, accompanied by shared giggles. Robert glared down the hall to find the source of the surely judgmental giggles. Jessica and her friend were returning from the pool, hair and swimsuits soaked and wrapped underneath towels. Robert responded with an annoyed glare as they sauntered down the hall.

"What are you two on about?" Robert asked as the two casually made their way down the hall.

"Nothing at all. You just look like you're going crazy down here," Jessica replied, her friend smiling behind her.

"No I'm not," Robert spouted incredulously.

"Then why have you been pacing back and forth like you're going mental?" his sister asked.

"I'm just thinking; that's all," Robert responded.

"Thinking about that girl?" Jessica pressed.

"I don't know what you're talking about."

"I've seen you two sneaking off at the beginning of every party!"

"I've just been doing other stuff ..." Robert answered coyly.

"Okay," Jessica mumbled, unconvinced. "We're going to go get ready. See you around." She gestured down the hall before the two walked away.

Robert resumed his preparations, leaning back and trying to contain his hysteria. Every party for the last month, he'd slipped away with Sierra just as the night had begun, and as each week culminated into those late Saturday night parties, he'd wrapped himself around those few sentimental memories, supposing that every day with her afterward would be even better.

Sunset came just at the end of the hour, and in the dark hours of the evening, pairs of headlights streamed up the winding switchbacks that led to the secluded gates of North Haven. Robert casually watched from his bench underneath one of the grand hall's windows, trying to pick out which car she might arrive in. He glared out the window, transfixed, as cars overflowed the driveway with even pairs of silhouettes departed from them and strode up to the entrance. He patiently held this position for the next ten minutes and he still hadn't seen her.

"What's going on?" Sierra asked him.

"Oh, I'm just looking out the window," Robert said turning to her, rather startled.

"Looking for me?" she asked, beaming a playful smile.

"No, I was looking for that other pretty girl. I don't see her."

"Oh hush. So how have you been doing lately?" Sierra asked as the two started to head down the main hall toward the ballroom.

"I've been pretty good; just been a regular ol' week at North Haven" Robert replied "How 'bout you? How have you been?"

"Not too bad. I've just have had school all week," Sierra answered.

"Oh yeah? What's that like?" Robert asked mockingly.

"You're just going to do this all night, aren't you? And it's not like you don't have school too."

"No, I don't have to go to school. I get tutored," Robert corrected condescendingly. "But what *is* school like?" Robert asked, genuinely interested.

"You know … it's like school," Sierra tried to answer.

"No I don't know," he insisted. "I've done two years of school, and that was elven years ago."

"I guess it's probably like your tutoring, but I get out if the house every day and I see my friends every day," she tried to explain.

Robert nodded, pretending to understand.

By now, they'd made it to the ballroom with a large buffet lining the east wall. Robert handed Sierra a plate and then got himself one and began down the line of food, a servant eagerly following them on the other side serving them.

"I can't imagine what it'd be like to not go to school. Don't you get lonely up here just you and your family?" Sierra added.

"It's *never* just me and my family. Between the guests we always have staying with us and the army of servants, it's like we have our own city up here," Robert boasted. "And I don't really mind the silence."

She nodded in agreement.

"Uhh, I'll take the Alfredo please." Robert gestured to the fettuccini.

"And I'll take the same," Sierra added.

The servant diligently acknowledged the two.

"Very true, seeing that, when I first met you, you were running away from me!"

"I wasn't running away …" He tried to explain. "I have many guests to attend to! You stopped me."

"Aren't you glad I did, though? You might have been too busy 'greeting' people for us to properly meet each other," Sierra argued.

"I guess you're right, and I don't regret any of it!" Robert admitted with a smile.

The night drew on. And after dinner, the two, as they had every Saturday night since they'd first met, escaped to the most lonesome confines of the home, bickering back and forth about the same nonsense until it all came to a slow, predetermined ending, abruptly halting any connection for another week.

Robert and Sierra hid, stowed away in the upper east wing's servants' quarters playing a game of chess. Robert's black pieces dominated the board against the challenger. Sierra studied the pieces carefully and tensely, as if she was going to make a well-calculated move before asking, "What's the horse do again?"

"It moves like an L," Robert muttered for the hundredth time.

"Oh," she said, as if she had figured it out. She resumed her thought on her game-winning move before carefully placing the rook. Robert shook his head and tried not to laugh.

"What?" Sierra inquired.

"Look, you put yourself in checkmate." He gestured with his finger.

"Oh …" She said dumfounded. "Well, I'll just have to practice for next time, but you know what time it is."

Robert looked at his watch, seeing the dreaded time of 11:55. "Oh … you have to leave soon," Robert mumbled.

"Yeah I guess so," she agreed somberly. "I had a great time with you tonight."

"Yeah me too, and I guess I'll see you next week?"

"Of course! Just next week."

The two awkwardly looked at each other before Sierra opened her arms for a hug and Robert followed.

"I'll miss you," she mumbled into his shoulder.

"I'll miss you more." And as the two withdrew and looked each other in the eyes, Robert closed his eyes blindly, leaning in to kiss her before he quickly withdrew to her smiling.

"Good night," she said as she left.

"Good night," Robert mumbled.

CHAPTER 7

Carried Away

S ocial gatherings at North Haven were all too common. Frequented by the most disparate members of the elitist class, the estate was constantly brimming with guests. All who came from across the States for business were invited to Eugene's palace for endless feasting, world class hospitality, and a pleasant night's sleep. All at the expense of an ample amount of praise for the homeowner; and if this was too much, they weren't invited back. At any given time, five or more guests were staying at North Haven, with some sort of party following their arrival, set on the Friday or Saturday night and with all the region's wealthiest on the invite list.

It was on one of these random nights that Robert found himself once again in the ballroom surrounded by dancers, minglers, and the occasional heavy drinker. But this time, instead of avoiding all of them, he sat at one of the tucked away tables, alone and watched the wave of dancers spinning aimlessly, swept away by the directed undertow of the band's rhythm. Robert wondered if she was coming. She wasn't here yet, so would she show up at all.

"What are you looking at?" a familiar voice rang from behind him. It wasn't Sierra.

"Oh hi, Jess … and …." Robert began as, like always, he couldn't remember Jessica's new suitor's name.

"It's David," the he muttered lowly under his breath, as this had been the third time Robert had asked.

"So, where's your lady friend?" Jessica asked curiously, her tone raised an octave.

"What do you know?" Robert asked with a level of skepticism and defense befitting someone on trial for murder.

"I saw you two last time! When are you just going to come out and admit it?" Jessica demanded.

"I don't know what you're talking about," Robert lied with the most condemnable grin.

"Lie all you want, but you're not fooling anyone. Even Mom and Dad are asking about it," Jessica added, walking off with David.

Robert smiled at his sister and her insight despite his secrecy; he knew he could trust her but still didn't want to give her the satisfaction. A moment after the distraction passed, Robert returned to think about his pessimistic thoughts.

"Where is she?" he mumbled under his breath as he flicked his wrist to look at his watch. It was eleven after six. When he wasn't counting the ticks of his watch, he'd look up at all the dancers and talkers, expecting her to be wading through it all standing out so brilliantly that he could never miss her. But when he looked up, he saw only the prosaic scene of one of his father's parties. He just couldn't understand. They had planned to meet here and … It just didn't make sense at all.

Robert leaned back in his chair, taking a heavy breath and stretching his arms before recomposing himself. He couldn't wait here forever.

And he didn't. After another ten minutes of waiting, Robert's anxiety overtook any patience he had for waiting and instead, he began to wander about the ballroom. Maneuvering through the crowd, he began to pick apart each social circle just looking for her. A glimpse of what might have been her only teased and stirred his hope. And after a few sweeps through the ballrooms, peeling through spiraling circles of dancers and interlocutors, Robert saw her walking in with her family. Feeling embarrassed and obsessive, he slinked away back into the crowds and returned to his chair. Looking apathetic and, most importantly, cool, he sat lazily and carefree in his chair, as lackadaisical as any teenager would as she strutted up to him, taking a seat next to his.

"You're looking cool," she said with a hint of condescension and ridicule, allayed by the usual playful smile.

"I was just relaxing … waiting for you…" he added.

"I've never seen relaxing look so forced," she pointed out, and Roberts's face brightened to a rosy red pleading guilty to the crime. "I need to tell you something though," she mumbled with a slight sulking tone that warned of future dejection.

"What is it?" Robert's concerned voice broke out, refracting off the tension of the situation.

"Come; take a little walk with me," Sierra said as she stood up and began to walk away slowly, waiting for Robert.

Robert stood. With no alternative, and followed Sierra, aware that whatever she had to say could not be good. As he followed her down the hall, Robert's mind could only imagine the worst and all of it being his fault.

The two meandered out into the south lawn. The night had obscured any specific detail and coloring, leaving only blurred outlines in the darkness and highlighting the glowing glare that shined through the revealing windows of North Haven. As soon as she had found a spot that offered just enough privacy, she stopped and waited for Robert, who had fallen behind, confused and nervous.

"Are you coming?!" she asked, excited and impatient, the spirited wisp of her tone coiled around the significance of each word buoying up Robert's worry.

"I'm coming, but maybe if you just told me what was going on, I wouldn't ..." He stopped himself from appearing rash and apprehensive.

"You wouldn't what?" Sierra grilled, pushing Robert deeper into his problem.

He hated when she did this. "I ... wouldn't ..."—perturbation seethed out of each word as Robert struggled to find a confident ending to his last sentence—"be so nervous," he finally conceded, stripping himself of his self-imposed divinity.

"Oh, Robert," she began with a comforting smile that was lost in the dark. "I'm sorry. I just wanted to spend time alone with you."

"Oh," Robert said, looking down at his feet to hide his embarrassment He looked up to smile back at her but it was lost in the dark.

"Know anywhere were we can get lost?" Sierra asked, her hands luring Robert farther.

"I know where!" Robert answered immediately. He continued down the garden's path, his hand now leading Sierra's as the two headed down toward the fringes of the property between North Haven's estate and the unclaimed, woods that encroached the estate.

A clearing projected through the forest leading to a small dirt trail that no one on the estate seemed to know about but Robert. Dull, long days of being alone on the estate, and a banal family had led Robert to find this trail. He could only speculate that it was formed as a back road the home's builders used. He could never reach the end.

Robert led Sierra to the base of the trail and crouched and began to dig through a pile of leaves until he found what he was looking for—a lamp he kept stowed away on the side of the trail for any sort of night walk. He lit the old antique, and as a whisper of gas escaped the lamp, an intense kerosene halo glowed in its rusted crown and projected a translucent orange glow across the surrounding forest and Sierra's enchanted expression. Robert smiled brightly with the assurance that he knew the path.

Creeping along the trail as it squeezed itself within the clearing between the adventitious tree growth, he felt bold. As he led her through the trees, he romanticized a brave image of himself—sure and swift as he cast an illuminating light against the demented, precarious night. Sierra followed closely and subtly slipped her hand into his which only enlarged Robert's ego. A small clearing opened ahead as the dirt path led into a small pond with a curving, wooden bridge that climbed over the pond and met the same path where it continued on the other side. Robert, giving no regard to the interruption, continued seamlessly over the bridge, only to be stopped by his curious follower, who stood on the bridge looking into the water. The pond's edges were encircled by the woodland's tallest trees walling off the isolated mere.

"What are you doing?" he asked, a little annoyed by the interruption.

"Just looking," she said, her head peering over the calm water.

"C'mon, the place I wanted to take you is up ahead," he said, gesturing at her excitedly with a wave of his arm.

"Yeah, but I think this is good," Sierra replied, content with the marveling at the vista. Sierra sat down, dangling her feet off the bridge's open side and staring into the water's reflection.

Defeated, Robert backtracked and stood beside her as she looked out onto the water to maybe see what she saw. He sat down, setting the lamp next to her, and she soon nestled into his arms. Her spontaneous unpredictability put Robert on edge. Robert felt too emotionally invested to be prone to her designless actions and far too devoted to pull away.

"I just wanted to be alone with you; that's all," she said as she snuggled in a little tighter. No amount of pushing or shoving was going to let him escape even if he wanted to. Despite that this had been the closest he has ever been to Sierra, A foreboding feeling of loss haunted the moment. Robert had never seen her act like this before but didn't want to ask simply because he didn't want to know. The two sat on the bridge, detached and far beyond the notice of the joyous party of North Haven, finding peace in silent isolation.

As the night pushed onward, the gala wore down, losing its momentum, and the less rambunctious guests retreated to their cars or their rooms, leaving only the most diehard and drunken partiers in the ballroom to try and outlive the night. Before too late, Sierra and Robert returned, arriving just in time before Sierra was announced missing. Sierra said a good-bye to Robert after he kissed her good night and returned to her car. And as she walked out the room, he stared tenderly at her for as long as he could before she disappeared back behind the door she entered from. She must have known that he did this every week because she seemed to pace her stride as she walked out. She waited until she was the last one out, turned to wave goodbye and shut the door behind her. At the sound of the latch of the door, he dropped his wave but continued to gawk onward at the door. Even if she would be gone for another week, he knew that every moment between now and then would be spent reminiscing of every night they shared and planning every day he would get to spend with her. It was hard not imagining her in his definition of forever, but Robert pretended that he knew better than to get carried away by such naive ideas like love and forever.

"What are you doing, dear?" His mother interrupted his thought. He realized he had been lost in a trance of his own thoughts as he still stared at the door.

"Nothing at all! I got a little lost in thought!" Robert explained as quickly as he could before receding back into the home.

CHAPTER 8

Keeping Rhythm

Robert sat at his desk with his private tutor, Dr. Taft, who was rambling about something else now. He wasn't paying attention. Normally he would, but Robert's mind was focused on more important things. Intermittently, Robert tuned in and out of the lesson plan and while most of it he chose not to hear, he could anticipate that Dr. Taft was going to go off on another needless tangent about the "fascinating uses of right triangles"

Dr. Taft was one of the most revered private tutors in all the East Coast, brought out by his father and now one of the many non-Motter residents of North Haven. Having taught all the Motter kids individually for all of their childhoods, Dr. Taft had made a small fortune out of it, including a rent-free mansion. Each weekend, he would use whatever absurd amount of money he'd earned and would travel to the city to spend it all on alcohol, gambling, and whatever other debauchery his money could buy, always returning Monday morning hungover and incoherent but ready to teach. He was pretty incoherent most days anyway, rambling on about nonsense and adding his own plot twists to history or criticizing everything that he taught out of the book but still relying on it to teach. Most days, Robert paid attention, knowing how important it all was despite the professor's added opinions, but today, he found his mind going astray, thinking of her.

"Triangles! They are a thing of Beauty." Taft would begin trying to contain his excitement. "If you were to tell me just 3 things about a triangle I could tell you all the rest! Who his drinking buddies are, what his favorite color is but most importantly I could tell you the other measurements of its sides and its corresponding angles," Dr. Taft began as he sketched out a right triangle across the wheeled-in chalkboard. "Do you remember our good friend Pythagoras?" he asked with no response.

Robert sat inattentive, rolling his pencil across the table. Dr. Taft had not noticed until now because he had been too captivated in his own lesson plan. "Robert, I don't believe you're paying attention;otherwise, you would be absolutely absorbed by the wonders of triangles."

Robert, hearing this, smiled at his professor but still focused on his pencil. "Sorry, Dr. Taft. I'm just thinking about other things."

"Well that's not like you at all. Thinking? And worst of all, not thinking about the geometric wonders of life? What crimes against humanity are you devising in that rudimentary mind of yours?" Dr. Taft inquired in his usual overdramatic fashion.

"A girl," Robert painfully admitted.

"A girl!" Dr. Taft repeated with hysteria. "And I suppose you think a girl is more important than the laws of geometry that form the building blocks for all architecture and are a fundamental part of higher math?"

"Maybe," Robert remarked dubiously, knowingly provoking the doctor.

"Well, maybe you're right,"

"I am?" Robert asked since his opinion was usually wrong in the Doctor's opinion.

Dr. Taft conceded. "There's not much to all of this without love," he gestured to the math written on his chalkboard.

"What do you know about love? You're not married!" Robert commented.

"I know more than you do!" Dr. Taft scoffed. If Robert were in arms reach, he surely would have smacked upside the head. Dr. Taft eyes returned to fix a judging glare on the boy. Dr. Taft always had a serious tone that dominated and intimidated those new to him, but the occasional helpless smile at his own comments hinted at his playful nature. Despite his own personal shortcomings and his questionable pedagogic style, he was a fine teacher and one of the only people Robert considered his friend. "Understand at least this; do not let the special people in your life slip past you," He preached with heavier emphasis with each word that followed. "If anything, let that be the lesson for today. You work hard, unlike Jack," he added scornfully. "You can have the day off to go think about this girl of yours and how you're going to woo her next time you see her."

Robert, wide-eyed and with no questions asked, accepted the gift with a smile. He grabbed his notebooks and headed out of the classroom. Dr. Taft watched him leave, smiling to himself, and went back to looking out the window, where he saw not the outside but an escape from a reminder of his youth.

Robert walked down the empty halls of North Haven under a new daylight. The whole day ahead of him seemed to brim with limitless potential, and he couldn't even imagine what to do with all that time. He took a seat on one of the benches that intermittently lined the great hall, trying to center his thoughts; however, all he could think about was her. Overanalyzing every detail from the night before, he imagined how well it had all gone. He stopped himself and recalled Dr. Taft's request to use today to think of how he would woo Sierra. It sounded like such a novel idea; how to win a girl's heart. He took a moment to think but it didn't take that long for him to suddenly realize what to do. The solution had been so apparent he couldn't object to it in anyway and it would— without a doubt— work. Robert made his way to the storage room where he and Sierra had spent their first evening together.

There, he pulled out the unaccounted piano that Sierra had so keenly found that fateful night. Robert was going to express himself in the best way he knew, a love song. He began aimlessly pressing the keys until settling for a combination he liked. He had never written a song before, but he understood how individual notes complimented the other, each combination expressing a movement of emotion in a regard different than the last. And through these combinations, he could tell a story not limited by the specifics of words. Before this, writing a song had seemed absolutely pointless, for how could his creation possibly stand up in comparison with the greater works? So Robert had stuck with what he knew. But now, the idea set in that his relationship with Sierra would be decided by the composition of one good song, and he had to fully commit himself to this endeavor.

He pressed the keys until a few lucky key strokes led him to the melody he was looking for. He then began to expand on it through the addition of chords and bass. And within the four hours gifted to him by his teacher, he'd created a basic melody and a small amount of accompaniment. Robert had never found so much devotion in himself, and he lost focus only when his wrenching gut reminded him what time it was.

He reached his arms out, stretching and popping his fingers, his first quick break. He sat up straight and stretched his back and arms before walking out of the boiler room. In the hall just outside the auditorium, the far-off figure of Jessica shouted, "There you are! C'mon, Robert. You're twenty minutes late for dinner!"

A surprised "oops" slipped out, and Robert, wracked by guilt, doubled his previously relaxed pace to catch up with his sister.

"Where were you?" Jessica asked, mildly peeved that her brother had made her and everyone else wait for dinner.

"Nowhere," Robert replied vaguely.

"Well, you're late and everyone's been looking for you."

His mouth moved to sound out a less audible "oops," and Robert continued silently down the hall reproached by his guilt.

After dinner, he returned to the aloof piano. He worked with high esteem, admiring his own self-discipline. She would undoubtedly be his after she'd heard the emotion he'd put into the composition. The night growing overhead did not still the hand that dabbled across the piano. And as the echoes magnified through the halls of New Haven, Robert would remember, above all, the distortion of the empty notes as his melody caromed off the corridors into a hollow existence.

CHAPTER 9

Sierra on a Tuesday

On Tuesday, a massive delivery of food, liquor, medicine, clothes, mail, and whatever else the Motters had collectively ordered the previous week was scheduled. A massive engine rumbling from the steep hillside warned of the truck's arrival five minutes ahead of time. Pulling up to the east entrance in a crooked and careless maneuver, the driver, along with a team of three other men directed by a foreman, unpacked themselves from the cramped truck cabin and began to unload disparate assortment of crates and barrels, dispersing the goods throughout the home in their appropriate places.

The foremen delivered the mail, sorting through stacks of mail and tediously organizing it into the twenty mailboxes on the side entrance of the home, one for each family member, servant, and whoever else decided to stay at North Haven for a prolonged period of time. Unloading usually took an hour or longer. Robert strayed above from the overlooking walkway, feeling forced to watch as the invasive commotion distracted him from anything else he might do. A wheeling of dollies, shuffling of footsteps, and the barking of orders summarized this weekly interruption. And all Robert could do was watch from the balcony of the side foyer as the men tracked their disruption through the entire home.

By the end of it all, Eugene would meet with the foremen, going over a receipt of all the delivered goods. Robert admired how keen and calculating his father was, having servants check to guarantee the shipment was received in full and bluntly pointing out any mistakes. This would be followed by demands of reimbursement or threats of termination of service, forcing the foreman to avoid any possible mistake, understandable or not, while dealing with Eugene. His father's fearless approach when it came to strangers shrinked Robert's own ego.

Robert had, for the most part, ostracized himself from the rest of his family the past week, composing his love song deep within the home's clandestine storage room and surfacing only for food and the forced schooling. He perfected and reperfected each piece of the song that he imagined would be fundamental to winning Sierra's heart.

With a decisive signature on the foreman's clipboard, Eugene signed off the hour-long dealing, and the foreman began shouting orders for his team's exit—which was just as noisy as their arrival. The weekly distraction was enjoyable for a change. Robert had appreciated the excuse to get away from his piano. Robert's fingers ached and his head rung with pain, overwhelmed by the perpetual repetition of previously failed melodies running through his mind. Eugene made his way up the stairs after his dealings were over and met Robert perched over the railing.

"The foreman says you've got letter," Eugene said, stopping in front of his reclusive son who he had not seen all week.

"I did?" Robert responded, surprised. He didn't know anyone outside of North Haven or at least anyone who would send him mail.

"I don't know," Eugene replied apathetically with a shrug of his shoulders. "By the way, where have you been lately? The servants say they only see you at dinnertime."

"I've just been doing stuff," Robert replied, hiding so openly behind his vagueness.

"Whatever," Eugene replied. "Did you hear about your sister's proposal? I know you've been too busy doing whatever it is you do to pay attention to your family," he scoffed as he passed Robert up the steps.

Robert remembered his sister being excited about a proposal a few weeks ago but had forgotten in the absence of the usual, constant reminders that were given to him by his family. He left for his room and dug through his nightstand, looking for a key he had set aside randomly eight years ago when, at the time, it had seemed pointless for an eight-year-old to have a mailbox. Shuffling aside papers, trinkets, and other misplaced things, Robert found a little, brass key stashed away beneath it all. He nearly ran back to the side foyer with the excitement of getting this unexpected little surprise delivered to him. He jammed the key in his appointed box and opened it to a single, carefully placed envelope.

Its insignificant size was surprising; in his mind, he'd imagined something more promising. Having it physically demeaned to a single letter was just a little disappointing. He reached for the envelope, addressed in the standard manner and sent from a place he didn't know; the only identity tied to it was the neatly scripted

"Robert" written in calligraphy addressing it. He peeled off the wax seal and pulled out a written letter.

Dear Robert,

I wanted to apologize ahead of time of what for what I'm about to say. When I first saw you, your obvious efforts of hiding were funny, and I couldn't help but get to know the person lost in the crowd. It's kind of how I called you out and was so persistent about meeting you. I'm glad I did, as I would never have gotten the chance to have known such a sweet, interesting person as you. And frankly, if I hadn't stopped you, you might still be wandering around that ballroom trying not to look lonely. Then over the next few months I couldn't stop thinking about you, and coming to your father's parties became all I looked forward to. And now this is where I need to apologize.

I'm afraid last Sunday will be the last time I will get to see you for a while. I wanted to tell you then, but I was too nervous and didn't want to ruin the evening with the overcast of bad news. I'm sorry, Robert, but my family and I are moving down south, too far to be able to see you every week. I don't even know when I might see you next. I should have told you that night. I hope you can understand and please write me back.

Sincerely yours,
Sierra

Robert read on incredulously more so doubting the authenticity of the paper. But the more he read, the more true it seemed to be. Questions pestered and scratched in his head about all the things she didn't tell him until now. He read again, trying to find answers to these questions between the text, but in the letter's limited, vague wording, he only found the one; she left him. Still, his mind clung to the significance of each word, trying to find something more in between the lines. It wasn't until he noticed what the last line had read that he knew what to do.

He took the letter upstairs to his room, where he could maybe put down on paper the unanswered questions he had left. He stared at the letter set standing open on its folds with a blank piece of paper in front of him and a pen in hand that hesitated to touch the paper. He thought about what Sierra's letter had said and how best to respond. He hated the idea of not talking to Sierra and having only one opportunity to resolve all his problems. After much consideration, he began to write out "Dear Sierra, Why didn't you tell me before?" just before a bitter insecure thought convinced him to throw it off the table and start over. He couldn't be so unwelcoming. A few more tries and a lot more thought gave him this:

Dear Sierra,

The past few months have been the most memorable of all my life. I don't get the pleasure of meeting, nor do I have the courage to meet, very many people, but I'm glad you forced me to know you. I'm happy you didn't tell me that night. The night would have been more heartbreaking and bitter if I had known about the looming complications. It's sad to see you leave, and I could never imagine not seeing you again. I hope we can meet again someday. Enjoy your new life and thanks for meeting me.

Sincerely,
Robert

That was all he could manage.

He couldn't imagine their relationship lasting through only letters. It was hard to understand that something that had —in an instance— moved into the core of Robert's life would be disappearing without warning the next day. He hastily sealed the letter.

The foreman and his crew were leaving; if he didn't deliver the letter now, he would have to wait a week. Running through the hall with a less-than-graceful stride that ended in him tripping down the stairs, Robert gave the letter to the foreman, who hadn't moved since Robert had left to go upstairs. He looked at Robert with a bothered, judgmental look as he picked the letter out of Robert's hand and returned to his clipboard.

Robert walked away from the clearly busy warden. He wondered what to do with himself. The thought of the past few months having ended so instantly disheartened him. He resumed his early post on the stairs and thought of all his self-imposed miseries. He thought of the song he'd spent all week composing and how all that effort had suddenly been rendered pointless. Now he didn't really need to finish the song. But he was so close to finishing. And it was so good he could not imagine giving it up.

Robert almost leaped from his miserable seat before realizing there was no rush; he could do it tomorrow. Robert slouched back for a moment, enjoying his own belittlement. Looking out into the empty foyer, he saw that he was the only one there now. The echo of the truck's noisy clatter grew faint with its return to civilization.

Chapter 10

Outlines from Before

J ordan read the letters from Sierra to Robert—thirteen letters telling only half a story and leaving the prier to extrapolate the words that had been written in between each new letter. Here was a love story of two people divided, living apart, fed by the composition of enduring endearments—"I miss you"—and hopeful words; "I can't wait to see you again someday!" The last letter announced no forewarning of trouble between the two and was only a cutoff in the conversation.

"Where are the other letters?" Jordan asked as she looked farther under the bed, finding no sign of the rest of the love story. Annoyed with the lack of conclusion, Jordan gave up looking but assumed she would find the rest of the letters elsewhere. "So Robert lived here," she said, continuing to talk to herself and secretly hoping that someone would include him or herself in her conversation. "That explains one person in the picture," she added, looking at the picture from the nursery. Jordan assumed Robert was the older man in the photo.

She sighed; the little bits of concrete evidence she had found still drew an incomplete picture of the past residents.

Jordan left Robert's room to head back to go look for some other lost history. She carried the letters back with her. The light faded with the impending night coming at its scheduled time. She headed through the halls, passing the line of doors that followed her on her left. Empty corridors forced her to stop and check for anything animate, but she saw only the movement of shadows, which further fed her paranoia. Creeping around every corner seemed to always be another. It seemed only by chance that Jordan had found the door leading to Robert's room; she could only imagine what else might be hiding out of sight.

Jordan's thoughts were interrupted by a creaking footstep that echoed down the halls. Jordan stopped in her stride to maybe catch the lurking specter and found only hollowness standing in its place. Blaming the wind for the interruption, she looked back at the letters. This one lone piece of evidence about the truth behind this place seemed to tease Jordan. She looked at the music notes one last time, wondering what the story was behind the faded ink lines of the crumbling paper.

Ten minutes of aimless wandering led her nowhere that she hadn't already found. In fact, she was almost back where she had started, the auditorium.

She entered the back way, where she had originally entered. The auditorium, unchanged by the transition of the day, was, as always, blindingly black. The bright ray of her flashlight only brightened the somber glory, lighting the dull colors of the already black wall and the rusted seats. She could imagine a full house, each seat filled with an audience member teetering on the edge of their seats as the play came to its gripping climax. The auditorium's glory days had long passed, and now the only entertainment it provided was wondering what might have been.

Jordan hopped up on the stage, the entire room focalizing on her. She looked out to where there might have been a crowd and screened the seats with her flashlight, half hoping someone would be amid the many seats watching. But as Jordan expected, no ghosts were there to watch a play. She continued looking around to the back to see what she could find. On the far east wall in the backstage, a ladder accessing the catwalks hung down like a forgotten back door to heaven. The rest of the backstage was empty. Jordan looked around at the unscuffed floors and the lack of any props or instruments. Like the rest of the home, this place was removed of anything that might have been here, and she shouldn't have been surprised.

She continued through the backstage area, segueing into what she figured was a maintenance hall, given that, instead of the gilded halls that spanned most of the home, it was a narrow, brick tunnel with wires lacing through its walls. An insignificant door was at either end of the hall, and at random, Jordan headed toward the one on her right. To no surprise, it was some sort of storage room. Metal shelving cluttered the room, with paint cans, tools, and sundry other things. Two large boiler vats hid behind the mess in the back, almost touching the ceiling, and sprouted large piping that rooted into the walls. It was amusing to see what was left behind. Jordan looked through all the odd little things she could find. Even when someone lived here, they probably forgot this room existed, she thought, meddling through a toolbox. And after realizing there wasn't anything in here, Jordan left to go check the other room.

The other storage room was almost an identical mess. She was looking through the shelves before noticing chalk drawing on the wall behind it. Cute children's drawings were all along the lower part of the wall, just within a child's reach. She saw teardropped faces and mingling stick figures, all the lines crudely drawn and not meeting the beginnings of others. However, among the crude drawings were a few well-drawn images—the behind of an elephant walking away, a cat in midstride, and a parakeet on a branch—all spread randomly among their less elegant counterparts. The chalk outlines had been fainted by age but were still easily visible against the dark, concrete wall.

Each drawing was completely whimsical compared to the home and didn't seem to belong. The home lacked any defining personal items, but to see something that was so personal as these simple drawing seemed surreal. Jordan bent down to touch unable to believe their authenticity. The chalk rubbed off with the stroke of her finger, paling the already faint line.

She looked around the room, searching for anything else noticeable. There, behind one of the shelves, protruded some sort of large wooden cabinet tucked behind one of the shelves—a piano. She pulled it out with excitement and lifted the key guard. Preserved, despite negligence, all the keys were intact and each, although flat, played its respective note or something close to it. She played little tunes that she knew, ignoring the discordant sound before asking herself the obvious question. What was the piano doing here?

She stopped mid note to think about it. She thought that maybe it was for the auditorium but shook her head. The path to the auditorium was too far and too difficult to get to with this piano. She couldn't think of any explanation, other than that someone had found peaceful solitude in this hidden room and had come here to play in the harmonies of silence.

It had dawned on Jordan at this point that what was still left here, in this room, was what was left unappreciated and forgotten. The room was filled with oddities that no one could be bothered with remembering about. Much like the room, this palace housed a forgettable moment in time that clearly no one really cared to remember.

CHAPTER 11

Living between Letters

Tuesday was Robert's second favorite day of the week. He listened from the stairs for the noisy truck to trumpet its loud, song over the mountain's switchbacks. There he waited, letter in hand, as the foreman and his crew began to unload their goods.

"Here. Can you deliver this?" Robert said, handing the foreman a letter with "Air Mail First Class" stamped in intense red ink. The foreman looked down at the letter, stamped with postage equal to half of his day's pay. He glared at Robert, who was too impaired by his nervousness and excitement to notice the foreman's judgment.

Every Tuesday, the foreman would come to deliver his letter, and every Saturday, at the oddest hours of the day, another servant would go out to the city to pick up the mail and other odds and ends that had accumulated since the foreman's last delivery. Robert would write Sierra on Monday and have his letter delivered on Tuesday. He would read and reread her letter periodically through the week, attempting to shorten the emotional distance

A Nocturne of Echoes

between them. It was difficult not to be a little bit disappointed by how their relationship had devolved to this. He hoped their bond would only grow stronger over the months. But despite his efforts, the letters had been only been a lifeline, a letter a week, barely enough to consider what he had with Sierra a relationship. Robert knew of the complications of only getting by with letters and would try and fill them with as much hope and promise as he could wedge in between each sentence. He spoke of an inevitable future in which they saw each other again, "I can't wait to see you," and weighed the statement down with, "I miss you." And for the most part, Sierra would respond with the same hopeful affirmations, both speaking hollowly of a promise caving in by its lack of a solution. The letters would have to do for now, as Robert tried to figure out how to fix this relationship's sentence to doom.

Robert watched as the laborers brought in more than their usual shipment. Five trucks had come this week with a crew of more than thirty unloaders. Crate after crate of food was brought in, along with boxes of silverware and plates, and a river of beautiful, white roses by the hundreds poured in on the arms of the grimy laborers. Table clothes and napkins, along with a full-sized table were all being moved into the home. Jessica's wedding was only a few days away, and her dad did not spare any expense. Robert's eyes followed the busy workers as they shuffled through the home carrying tables or armfuls of goods.

Robert's eyes weren't the only ones watching. The vigilant wedding planner watched with a scornful eye as the laborers, in his eyes, carelessly handled each piece of the wedding. Robert couldn't imagine how much money his father had paid for all of

77

this. Whenever he talked about Jessica's suitor—David, right?—he would go off, boasting about what a great son-in-law he was going to be and always esteeming him in the highest manner. He never talked so fondly about either Robert or Jack as he did David. Robert leaned over the balcony's railing, continuing to watch the unavoidable distraction. Eugene walked up behind him and joined him at the side of the rail.

"Are you ready?" Eugene asked his son as he looked down at the workers marching like ants with loads in hands toward the ballroom.

"Yeah," Robert responded. "Are you?"

Eugene laughed heartily at his son's intuition. "Not really," he replied as soon as his laugh had diminished to the point that he could speak.

"Why? You seem to like this guy, David, right?" Robert asked, also trying to confirm the groom's name.

"Yes ... David is a great man—a successful man—but it still doesn't give me comfort that I am giving my only daughter away in just a few days," he replied, anguished by his own sentence. "You just don't understand, Robert. Receiving the greatest blessings of your lifetime and having it about to be taken away from you; you know of this inevitable day, but you just never see it coming," Eugene added, looking at his son, who still looked confused. "You can't understand it now, boy, but someday you'll have to do the same thing. The greatest disparity among man is how much more a parent loves their child"

The concept still eluded Robert, but he could understand his father's idea of someday knowing anguish.

"By the way, a lot of the family will be here," Eugene digressed, "as well as many other important people."

"Okay," Robert replied. "I know."

"Just don't go hiding while they're all here. I don't care what you do while it's just us, but I don't want to be asked why my son is so weird," Eugene said bluntly.

"Okay," Robert responded a little more sullenly than he intended. Eugene slipped away to the nearby hall, leaving Robert with a question that he could never dare ask. Was his father ashamed of him? He shook his head incredulously, denying any of the obvious hints before eventually believing he didn't even care.

Robert headed up to the library, were he knew he could find his mother. Each family member was always at polar ends of the home in comparison with each other. Robert's mother, Pearl, always secluded herself in the library whenever no one was visiting the home. Jessica typically escaped from the home with her fiancé. And Jack had been at Oxford for the past three years studying business. In a year, Robert would follow suit for his freshman year and get the opportunity to watch Jack graduate. Going off to college had been such a faraway thought for Robert, and leaving his current life behind seemed too precarious compared to how he's been living.

Robert made it to the northern hall just steps away from the library. Having never seen his father so emotional in his life, he had convinced himself that he should probably check on his mother. The library was a sprawling, open room compared to the narrow, compact hall. Its high-ceilinged roof opened toward the sky; towering bookcases brimmed with both worn and immaculate books, the latter never touched for the uninteresting topics within them. Volumes of books about tax laws and stocks and bonds and numerous encyclopedias lined the rows of shelves numerically, descending from right to left by volume. Multiple copies of the same book varying only in edition were found above and below their previous editions.

And amid all this ignored knowledge was a single bookcase in the back right corner next to the most used chair in all of North Haven. It contained all his mother's past reads, bindings stretched and covers worn, books that weren't just for display. To his surprise, the most worn chair of the home sat vacant.

Robert looked quizzically at the chair, his mind stuck as he pondered where else his mother might be. "Not in here," he remarked pointlessly to himself. He left the library and started down the hall, until he ran into one of the servants coming around a corner doing one of his cleaning sweeps through the east wing.

"Hey, Joe, have you seen my mom?" Robert asked the obviously preoccupied servant.

Joe was an older man, probably in his late fifties, who had worked at New Haven ever since they family had first moved in. Wracked by age, Joe wobbled sporadically around the home with his cleaning cart trying to find a mess in the mostly unused home.

"No, I haven't seen her around. Sorry, friend," Joe replied, stopping to address the wandering child. While most servants of the home secretly despised the Motters for their stingy oversight over everything, Robert's father the guiltiest of this, Joe appreciated the work and free living that New Haven provided, making Joe easily the friendliest servant in the home.

"Oh, that's okay. Thanks anyway,"

Robert continued only a few steps down the hall until the familiar voice of the person he'd been looking for called out behind him.

"Robert, were you looking for me?" Pearl asked, peeking her head out of Jessica's room just as Robert was walking by.

"I was. How did you know?" Robert asked, surprised by her mother's seeming omnipresence.

"Well, the door was open, and you and the janitor weren't exactly quiet," she replied.

"Oh," Robert said, in an effort to save himself from his lack of insight.

"So, what did you need?" Pearl asked, attentive as usual to her son's issues.

"Oh right!" Robert had forgotten. "Nothing, I just wanted to see how you were doing."

His mother gave him a skeptical, incredulous look. "I was wondering when I would finally have a loving son!" she replied sarcastically, opening her arms for a hug in celebration of Robert's newfound love for his mother.

"Uh, no, Mom, that's not really why," Robert objected, hugging his mother anyway. "You know I love you."

"I know, but it's just not like you to come see your mother."

"Yeah … well … I just wanted to see how you were handling the upcoming wedding. Dad seemed pretty upset, so I just wanted to make sure you were doing okay."

Pearl let out a mournful sigh in response to her son's insight. "It is an inevitable tragedy—a parent losing her child to life. And I cannot say I'm not overtaken by it," Pearl explained.

Robert watched and listened silently to his mother's insight.

"But your father failed to see the warnings leading up to the day when life would take her away. The wedding is really just the culmination of Jessica's relationship with David, and their previously subtle relationship slipped by Eugene's attention, turning it into a surprise when David did propose to Jessica."

"Huh," Robert let slip as a rudimentary reflection. The wedding had kind of surprised him too, for just a couple weeks earlier, Robert had finally learned the guy's name. "By the way, what are you doing in Jessica's room?"

"Oh, just looking back at the past," Pearl remarked.

"Well, all right, I guess I'll let you escape back to the past then," Robert concluded, leaving his mother to her past.

Continuing down the hall, he reflected on all his mother said. His father chose to ignore the obvious signs that the day he would lose Jessica would come and really, he couldn't blame anyone but himself when he finally lost her.

CHAPTER 12

The Wedding

F riday morning, usually a time of serene harmony, had been overtaken by a wild bustle of guests and workers, all under the spell of the enchanting cascade, white flowers and cloth streamers overhanging the halls and foyers. An entire chapel had been unpacked and arranged in glorified beauty in the rolling, green pasture just behind the home around a belvedere that would see the beginning of a new marriage.

Robert watched out his bedroom window, adjusting his tux and tie, and stared with envy as workers adorned the aisle with bouqets of flowers set upon pedestals with cloth streamers strung in between them, parting a sea of benches to make way for a bride and groom. The notion of a wedding fascinated Robert--the moment of ultimately committing yourself to your partner for life. It was the last step love could ever take but not the end of its enduring journey. Robert had never been to a wedding and had only heard of the thought and work put into the celebration. But he could never have imagined all the facets of grander inlayed within every detail. Beyond that, Robert had not yet imagined that his sister was being wedded and was destined soon to leave the seclusion of North Haven.

Robert finished fidgeting with his tie and stepped down from the window. He was no stranger to tuxes, but this white one he was forced to wear for the wedding was just a little too snug, and he continued to constantly readjust his jacket. He took a quick look in a standing mirror, posing to look even more dashing. If only Sierra could see him right now. He headed downstairs, passing estranged aunts and uncles and even more elusive strangers all loitering in the main hall.

"Robert!" an excited voice called, stopping Robert midpace. This would be the first of many such calls, after which, he would be descended upon by a random family member in near sprint coming at him, arms wide, ready to sweep him away.

"Hi, Aunt … Mary," Robert responded, interrupted by a firm squeeze.

"How have you been?!" she replied eagerly with a grand smile, her enthusiasm belittling Robert's own lack of delight.

"Oh, I've been well. How about you?" Robert replied, trying to share his family member's excitement with a mutual smile.

"Good! Good! Just excited to see Jessica get married!" Mary replied.

A reserved figure stayed a few steps back from Mary; Uncle Walter remained more composed and elusive than his wife, hiding behind the dignity of his masculinity.

"Robert," Walter interjected briefly, extending his hand in regard for proper etiquette.

"Hello, Uncle Walter," Robert replied, a little daunted by his uncle's cold facade.

"So, Robert, where is your father? I have to give my brother a great, big hug!" Mary interjected, purposely interrupting Walter's awkward reunion.

"Sorry, I don't know. I think he might be in the ballroom," Robert replied.

"Oh, that's okay. I don't mind taking a look for him in *your* wonderful home!" Mary replied with a pleasant, subjective laugh.

The two wandered farther down the west wing, despite the advice Robert had given them. He was at least happy they were gone; having only actually met his Aunt Mary and Uncle Walter a handful of times, Robert felt awkward whenever occasion forced an obligatory display of love for his distant relatives. Family seemed to lay in wait among the small clusters of mingling people, ready to descend upon Robert with deviating jabber. Not that he didn't appreciate his family, he just did not know them as well as he should have. Robert headed to the ballroom to continue to look for his father. The ceremony would start in just a few hours, and Robert was supposed to meet with him and his mother just before the ceremony.

Shoved in the corners and edges of the ballroom, guests lined the walls and tables, talking and meeting. Some Robert knew to be his family and friends of the family, and others were complete strangers. He could only assume them to be part of David's family but; then again, strangers weren't an uncommon sight in North Haven. He saw his father scattered among the groups of people, rambling to some of his friends in a corner with a glass of scotch in his hands and a brilliant grin on his face. He seemed to be sharing a laugh with the two other gentlemen surrounding him.

"Hey, uh, Dad, when did you want to meet with Mom?" Robert asked, awkwardly making his way into the group.

"Hmmm," Eugene sonorously hummed as he pulled out his pocket watch. "Looks like it's right around that time. We'll probably be seated for the ceremony in just another hour. Come on." He waved his hand, beckoning Robert to follow as he excused himself from the group. Eugene's previous dread of the wedding day seemed to have lapsed, replaced by a happy grin and an unusually pleasant attitude.

"So you seem happy about the wedding," Robert mentioned as the two casually strolled down the hall.

"Well ... I am still just a little heartbroken to see my daughter finally all grown up, but I think I found a way for it all to be okay," Eugene added optimistically.

"Well that's good," Robert replied plainly. Eugene never meddled with emotions around Robert, in an effort to maintain his stoic apparence, and actively encouraged Robert to do the same. "Emotions show that at any moment you can be vulnerable, and people will take advantage of that!" Robert remembered him once saying to hush his crying. And although Robert loved the inspiration of emotion, how could he argue with his father and his success in life?

The two went upstairs in the west wing and headed to Jessica's room. Pearl wanted to have a final moment all together just before the wedding—which Robert felt would be in vain, with his brother still at Oxford for another semester of school. As they opened the door, they saw two women applying makeup and fixing Jessica's hair in front of a mirror, reflecting her face toward the door, with Pearl back in the corner overseeing the perfecting of her daughter. A long, white, lavish dress hung on the nearby wall. Pearl did not acknowledge the two entering, and Jessica just gave them a quick glance with her eyes through the mirror's reflection.

"So, how is it all going? How do feel, Jessica?" Eugene asked, his tone subdued by his protective worry.

"I'm really excited!" Jessica mumbled to the mirror, trying not to move her mouth as one of the stylists brushed over her face with makeup.

"No cold feet? Nothing?" Eugene asked.

"No ... I mean the past few months I have, but I know now I'll be with someone who loves me and will always be able to take care of me." She continued. Eugene responded with a dubious look, which both Pearl and Jessica noticed.

"I know, dear. It seems just a little strange to me too," Pearl interjected.

"Well, you obviously had no doubt when you married me, right?" Eugene added.

"Of course, dear." Pearl smiled and glanced over at her husband before rolling her eyes as she returned her attention to Jessica.

The two stylists finished up and were excused to momentarily leave the room by Pearl. Jessica readjusted her chair so she could face the rest of the family.

"It's so strange to think that this will be the last time we will all be the same family," Pearl murmured to the awkward, unbearable silent tension of division that strained the intimacy between them.

"You know we'll always be family, Mom," Robert countered.

"You know I know that, but it will never be like it was as we divide and fray like the end of a rope; we'll always be connected but that won't stop the distance that grows between us. " Pearl said softly. And there was no arguing with that as the truthful silence continued to linger. "It's just too bad Jack couldn't come and join his sister for her wedding," she added.

"David is a good man, Jessica, and I hope you two have long, fulfilling lives," Eugene added weakly. "Well I, uh, have to go to my office before the wedding, to type something up. Come on, Robert, we'll let these two finish up."

Robert nodded, just as eager to leave as was his father.

"Good luck, honey. Have a wonderful wedding!" were the last words Eugene said to his daughter as he walked out.

For the upcoming ceremony, the scattered groups from across the estate converged on the chapel laid across the rolling green just beyond the reach of the eclipsing shadow of North Haven. Families and friends from both parties merged but divided themselves between the two columns of benches that hosted seats for the 150 guests in attendance, by Robert's guess. The large belvedere sat centered in front of the two disparate columns of people, with a small stage to its left hosting a string quintet anxiously waiting to play with their intruments at the ready. Finally settled, the band played an overture to the wedding—a peaceful, scaling melody that was the perfect prelude to a couple's pivotal moment.

David entered the belvedere on the right with the music playing, followed by the minister. Both stood under the arches as a parade of the dearest friends of the soon to be wed paced down the center aisle together. Robert stood in awe, perched at the edge of his seat, watching this single moment that held the bride and groom's most meaningful people coming together in support of their friends. David smiled and recomposed himself as his closest friends took him away from braving the loneliness under the arches.

Instinctively, Pearl stood up beside Robert, and the crowd behind her followed, forcing Robert to do the same. The prelude segued into the distinguished wedding march. In the center of the aisle, Eugene met his only daughter with a broken smile and a look of pride and took Jessica by the arm, leading her down the aisle to the slow rhythm of the wedding march. And at the end of the short march that symbolized the past twenty years of Eugene's life, he unwillingly gave Jessica to her new life.

The minister went into a lengthy prayer that meant nothing to Robert, addressing the tribulations and sacrifices that went into a wedding and then speaking of the unification of two lives, of two people making the ultimate commitment—to be together from this moment until an indefinite end. Making the final step of deliverance, Eugene gave away the bride.

"David and Jessica, you have made a decision in choosing to marry each other today," the minister said. "You are entering into a sacred covenant with God as life partners. Your marriage will be based upon your commitment to each other. You have been given the sacred duty of going forward from this day to build a strong relationship built on trust; responsibility; and above all, an undivided love for each other. We bless you this day and pray that you perpetuate this blessing throughout the eternity of your marriage by upholding your sacred duty to each other. You both have a responsibility to keep this blessing alive each and every day of your lives together. We wish for you the wisdom, compassion, and constancy to create a peaceful sanctuary in which you can both grow in love." The minister paused for a moment and looked at the couple; both Jessica and David seemed lost in thoughts of the wild future ahead.

"David and Jessica, have you come here freely and without reservation to give yourselves to each other in marriage?" the priest asked, turning now to the script.

"We have," the two responded.

"Will you honor each other as man and wife for the rest of your lives?"

"We will."

"David, do you understand and accept this responsibility, and do you promise to dedicate your life with unwavering certainty and fully committing yourself to creating a loving and happy relationship?"

"I do," David eagerly responded.

"And do you, Jessica, understand and accept this responsibility, and do you promise to dedicate your life with unwavering certainty and fully commit yourself to creating a loving and happy relationship?"

"I do," Jessica responded, reciprocating her soon-to-be husband's excitement.

"Since it is your intention to enter into marriage, join your right hands and declare your consent before God," the minister declared.

"I, David Curtis, take you, Jessica, to be my wife. I promise to be true to you in good times and in bad, in sickness and in health. I will love you and honor you all the days of my life."

"And I, Jessica Motter, take you, David to be my husband. I promise to be true to you in good times and in bad, in sickness and in health. I will love you and honor you all the days of my life."

"You have declared your consent before God. May the Lord in his goodness strengthen your consent and fill you both with his blessings. What God has joined, men must not divide. Amen." The minister's final declaration hung the weight of the anguishing path ahead for the newlyweds on those last fabled words, turning a promise of eternity into actuality, and David kneeled before Jessica, whispering some secret that only she should hear, and slipped the wedding ring on with the dazzling smile that only seemed to gurantee the promising future ahead of them. As he got up, Jessica returned the favor, slipping on the ring that sealed their union forever and symbolized their eternal love. A sonorous bang of clapping erupted from the crowd, with Robert eagerly joining in the commemoration of David and Jessica's love.

With a final closing prayer, the bride and groom walked down the main aisle, arms linked, leading the parade, with the best man and maid of honor following close behind and the rest of the congregation to follow. The formerly directed crowd, dissolved back to a mindless swarm of people flooding into the back entrances of North Haven, leaving behind them a mess of seats, confetti and flower petals across the previously organized chapel. The reception, scheduled immediately after the wedding waited, postponed by the lag of the crowd.

Most guests followed their designated seating arrangements, finding their artfully crafted name tags, while the less abiding grabbed a seat by their friends. But soon, everyone had found a seat at the tables encircling the ballroom, with the bride and groom and their wedding party given their special place high up on the stage. Commissioned waiters weaved in and out of the tables, taking orders for wedding meals and serving drinks, while commemorations for the marriage were spoken to the crowd. Robert sat at a table near the stage with his father and mother. The best man stood on the podium, rambling about some bygone golden days only he and the groom could relate to.

"I think I'm next," Eugene tried to whisper to Pearl over the loud best man.

"Are you nervous?" Pearl muttered.

Eugene looked at her for a second and readjusted himself in his chair. "A little," he admitted. "But I know just what to say!" he added no longer in a hushed tone, nearly interrupting the best man's speech.

With a general conclusion of the best, applause that cherished the moment ended his speech. The groom patted his best friend on the back, approving his words with a charming smile.

"Thank you, Jay," David said. "It's been a good run between the two of us, and I look forward to the years to come. I believe now the father of the bride has a few words to add to all that," David added, looking at Eugene, who snapped away from his personal conversation at the mention of his title.

Eugene rushed out of his chair and proceeded to the stage with an excited look. The groom was only afforded a customary handshake and smile before Eugen turned away from him to address the more important figure in the room, the audience. He manned the podium, standing straighter than his normally slouched back would prefer.

"When I first heard about the marriage," Eugene began, "I'll admit I was a little taken aback by the whole proposal. Losing my little girl was the last thing I ever wanted. As a father, I knew the day would come that some young, suave man would take my daughter from me. But I never thought it would be David," he said his voice full of praise as he stopped to look at the groom, who reacted with an approving smile. "David is a successful young man already, being a graduate of Harvard Business and owning several oil fields by the young age of twenty-four. I have no doubt that my daughter married a good man who will undoubtedly take care of her and her children. I haven't had the best opportunity to really acquaint myself with David, as he has usually been running off with my daughter instead of getting to know her father." He said jokingly with a collective laugh among the audience. "But when he asked for my blessings for the marriage, I knew I could trust this man based on his reputation and that of his family and all the accomplishments he has managed in his short lifetime. David, I would like to welcome you to our family, and by doing so, I would like to invite you to live here in my splendid estate of North Haven with Jessica as a third son of mine and an additional heir to my fortune!"

Eugene did the last thing he could do to still be with his daughter. He tried to bribe David into staying with the promise of a third of Eugene's wealth and the outstanding castle of his lost in the woods. Eugene looked back to David, who shared the same surprised look that the rest of the crowd did.

"Yes, of course!" David answered, standing with open arms to give his new father a hug.

Robert gawked at his father hugging his new third "son," baffled by what had just happened. It felt demeaning to Robert's own value as Eugene's true son, but Robert looked past the issue and only shook his head at his father.

The wedding concluded to every wedding's conventional ending, with the bride and groom enjoying a first dance together as newlyweds and their family and friends dancing with them in commemoration of this founding day of a new partnership.

Robert sat removed from the myriad of dancers, choosing to observe. Looking past the wedding, he watched the newlyweds dance. David led, and Jessica willingly followed him into whatever other dancer he would unintentionally crash into, a mishap he would amend with an affable laugh over his careless mistake. Robert smiled at the two and wondered what wonderful future the two would have, especially with David now living with them. Robert reflected back on the entirety of the wedding. A physical manifestation of the love between two people expressed with fields of flowers trimmed and displayed alongside a sundry of decorations in complimenting colors—all to delineate the lovers' intangible feeling towards each other. And throughout the entire occasion, Robert couldn't help but wish that Sierra was here with him.

CHAPTER 13

The Truth in Premonitions

Robert awoke Saturday morning to a recollection of the thoughts that had transpired over the past night—mostly of the meaning of love, the overwhelming feeling of deep affection for someone, and the ambiguous line between that feeling and simply liking someone that only the foolish would be so bold to cross. Robert lay in the same position he'd been in when he woke up, staring at the ceiling. With thoughts of love tied to Sierra, she crept into his mind, and Robert wondered what she was doing. And as the two subjects—love and Sierra—paralleled each other, the transparent question of whether Robert loved Sierra wandered into Robert's runaway train of thought. Did he love Sierra? Robert quickly shook his head in denial, quickly averting himself from being foolish enough to fall in love so quickly. But when would he cross the line? And what really decided that fondness for someone evolved it intolove?

He got out of bed, motivated by the pleasant thought of what was in his mailbox. He wandered out into the hall on which still hung half of yesterday's wedding decorations, either forgotten or neglected. Two servants checked in and out of rooms with food and wake-up calls for all of the guests who'd chosen to stay the previous night.

Robert had never seen every room full before. And his father's vision of having rooms for all who wanted to stay had fallen short when, the previous night, more than sixty people had wanted to stay but were turned away.

He headed down the cold stairs of the side foyer with his brass key in hand, anxiously rushing to the mailbox. He stuck his key in the hole with the confidence of knowing Sierra had written to him. He slid open the door to a different story. Locked inside the mailbox was nothing. In disbelief, Robert bent down to look inside the empty mailbox, unable to find the promised letter. Maybe the mail hadn't arrived yet. He withdrew himself from the empty mailbox and sent himself on a mission to redeem Sierra by finding the servant responsible for getting the mail.

Robert headed upstairs to the east wing's servant quarters, which took up roughly half of the upper east wing, with shared dormitories, bathrooms, and kitchens for the dozens of families who lived in only a quarter of the home. He walked into the small tasking office, where a chief butler hunched over a desk with a large pin board of keys behind him and a stack of payroll papers in front of him.

"Er ... excuse me, Sam?" Robert guessed, hating to interrupt the stranger.

"No ... but what did you need?" the chief butler asked helpfully, though not deviating from his paperwork.

"Did someone get the mail last night?" Robert asked timidly, going around any misunderstanding of a command.

"Yeah, Mary went out and got it last night," he replied, still unmoved by Robert's presence.

"All of it?" Robert asked desperately.

"As far as I know, we don't bring back only half of the mail," the chief butler replied, a slight overtone of impatience leaking into his words.

"Okay … Thanks," Robert responded and left the room with the disappointment knowledge that there was no letter this week. Maybe it had just gotten lost in the mail and he would see it on Tuesday.

As the week progressed, the strung-up evidence and welcomed witnesses of Friday's wedding dissipated, finally vanishing back into the classic state of North Haven by late Sunday afternoon. The final guests of the wedding had left, and Robert tried to distract himself over the weekend with his endless attempts at writing music, while continuously deviating into pessimistic thoughts about the missing letter. He thought only of the worse that could have happen.

And when Tuesday's inevitable dawning came, Robert checked the mailbox again, imitating the same excitement he'd had that previous Saturday morning, and encountered the expected surprise of the deep, vacant void of the empty mailbox. He shook his head in understanding, and with a solemn push, the mailbox door creaked to a close, locking the endless hope it had once promised inside.

But maybe she just didn't have time to write.

The defining moments of Robert's week vanished just as abruptly as they had come. The initial letters had been a surprise within themselves, something Robert now looked back on, reading half the story to which he had written the other half every week. It had now been delayed … for just a week.

The week passed, and that Saturday morning, he sprang from his bed, certain that a letter from Sierra would be in there. All the way down the steps of the side foyer, he reminded himself of this certainty, the undeniable truth that Sierra had written to him this week. But as he stared at the mailbox door, which harbored the real, forsaking truth, his bravery was diminished by the uncertainty of that closed door. He turned the key to the disappointing truth that there was nothing behind it.

Maybe his letter had gotten lost. Robert, comfortable with the possibility, proclaimed it be the truth and ran up to his room to write her a new one.

To Sierra,

I haven't heard from you in weeks! I've just been so preoccupied with the wedding I may have forgotten to write to you. Or my last letter got lost in the mail. But that doesn't matter. I just wanted to let you know that the wedding was fantastic, and I wish you could've been here.

Oh, Sierra, I've just been reminiscing about all the times that we have had together and just can't wait for the day when we can pick up where we left off. Every day I sit and ponder what life will be like when you are here, beside me, sharing thoughts and conversations about our lives and the wonderful people who fill them.

I hope everything is good down south, and like always, I am still missing you!

Sincerely,

Robert

Robert signed the letter with the content of knowing that now his relationship with Sierra would return to the feeble schedule of one letter a week. A creeping thought undermined Robert's content, asking him a simple question—why was he still even trying? Robert made every effort to ignore these pessimistic outlooks but couldn't help but humor the question. The truth was, Robert didn't really know why he was still trying.

Another Tuesday came, and Robert ritualistically handed the letter to the foreman, who usually bitterly snatched it from Robert's hand followed by a complaining grumble about the nuisance. Maybe he had done something with Robert's last letter.

"You've been delivering my letters, right?" Robert boldly asked.

"Of course. Why wouldn't I?" he sneered at Robert, who was convinced now it wasn't him.

"I don't know," Robert drawled, seeing the insecurity in his own question.

The foreman returned to his clipboard, leaving Robert excuseless as to the disappearance of his previous letter. But Robert continued to convince himself that something had happened to the last letter.

Robert patiently waited until Saturday morning, the pivotal moment when he would be assured everything was all right between him and Sierra. With the same enthusiasm and certainty he'd had the past few weeks, he checked his mailbox, confident that his last letter surely had been delivered. But the foreshadowing truth that filled the back of Robert's mind with doubt proved itself again. Something had to be wrong now. Robert futilely searched the mailbox, unable to find the missing letter. He solemnly shook his head, conceding at last to the fact that nothing was there. Maybe ...

Robert tried, but he couldn't find any culpability in anything other than Sierra. He withdrew himself incredulously from the mailbox without blame and promised himself that she would write back.

Tuesdays and Saturdays, Robert would triumphantly march to the mailbox with an unbridled hope that crumbled every moment he grew closer to the disappointing truth. It was always empty. It was during these next few weeks of insufferable ignorance and disconnection, Robert would attach himself to the only connection he had left with her, the song. It was through the begotten memories transcribed in the song, he could find some attachment and some hope for their relationship. But Robert, confused by dubious thoughts of optimism and dreading foretelling warnings of separation, only ever managed to sit at the piano bench. He considered it effort and thought that fate only kept Sierra away to motivate Robert to finish the song.

Three weeks after the first disappointment and under strife from checking the mailbox earlier that morning, Robert sat in front of someone else's piano in the solitude of the storage room with a blank musical score in front of him and inspiration fading into anxiety. Robert studied the last letter he had received, reading and rereading it and studying each word by itself and all of the words together, looking for ominous traces of this silence. But he could only find hope within the monotone words. He looked at the envelope it had come in and fixed on her address written across its front.

An obvious solution to all of Robert's problems had slipped past him every time he wrote to her. Mustering all his hope and courage, he ran out to the side foyer gate with the letter in hand. He stood within the night just outside of the faded light of the two porch lamps and looked out through the house gates to the entire world beyond North Haven. Robert squinted vainly at the address on the envelope as a reminder of where he would go. Driven by the same emotion that had crippled him the weeks before, he swung the gate open to the intimidating world outside of all that he knew. He stood motionless at the border line as his passions and fears tore him apart; pushed by his passion for this girl and dragged back by the harsh reality of not knowing what was at those ends. It was ultimatley the letter in his hand that had the only clue about what he could do. He looked back down at it and with a shameful step back he closed the gate. He had realized that he would be just as lost outside the gates of North Haven as he was here. At least here he could write her,

Robert trudged up to his room under the convincing sway of his own self-bolstered hope. He reminded himself that he was doing the right thing, no matter how minimal it seemed. He sat down at his desk, grabbed a sheet of paper and a pen and contemplated just what he should say. There couldn't be a chance that she hadn't read his past two letters.

Dear Sierra,

I haven't heard from you in nearly a month and was just curious as to how you were doing. I don't know how you've been lately, and I don't know if you received my last two letters. But I just wanted to let you know I have been trying to reach you and I hope you write back soon!

Like always, I'm still missing you, and I hope to hear from you soon!

Sincerely,
Robert

Robert felt embarrassed by how little the letter said and its general purpose. It was demeaning for Robert to have to remind her to write back and only emboldened the lingering, convincing notion that he should surrender to the disconnection. Robert tried not to look at those relieving, dreary thoughts and set the letter aside for Tuesday.

On Tuesday, Robert sent his next letter into the void of uncertainty, hoping for a sign back from the precarious darkness.

The following Saturday, he checked again, but his hopeful wish remained unfulfilled within the empty mailbox. And he checked back the next Saturday and again on Tuesday. Every week, he would face this same defeat, but would always be more than willing to check for a sign of hope.

And one day, just as he was about to face this regular defeat, he stopped himself just before unlocking the mailbox and withdrew his key from the lock. He looked at its masking door and felt satisfied with just that, choosing to ultimately wallow in the uncertainty of never knowing what it hid rather than to face the destined disappointment of learning there was nothing behind it. Robert backed away from the unopened mailbox, finally liberated by his own pusillanimity.

CHAPTER 14

Journey's End for Someone

T he sun blinked on the edge of the horizon, peering out with a bright gaze and projecting streams of bright, outstanding colors across the dim morning sky. The salient entry of the light through the west face of North Haven pierced tightly closed eyes that only wanted a few more moments of sleep. Jordan woke, squinting in the blinding light of the morning sunrise. Forgetting where she was, she had forgotten that she had chosen to spend the night in a stiff bed rather than her uncomfortable cot. She struggled out of the thick indent she had made in the mattress and frantically looked around the room before remembering she had fallen asleep in Robert's room. With a heavy sigh, she fell back in the bed, her back aching as it curved down to lean back on the stiff mattress.

Jordan headed back to her own room, braving the long, stagnant, cold corridors to gather her things and get ready for another day. She referred back to the sloppy map she'd drawn the other day, trying to make out what she had written. And when she had a vague idea of what she had drawn, she marked any room she hadn't checked. A large empty space vacated a quarter of the upper west wing with only a door leading into it, and Jordan, naturally curious, decided to head there first.

Tucked away in a small corridor that branched off from the main hall, she found a small, barely noticeable door with a small sign that reading, "Do Not Enter." And despite the suggestion, she entered anyway.

Opposing the sun-drenched halls outside it, the small, forgotten room remained in darkness regardless of the time of day. Jordan poked her head in, looking around in the indiscernible darkness before quickly falling back, gagging from the overpowering stench of mold.

She stood for a couple minutes at the door, allowing the stench to air out and rallying herself to face the repulsive smell.

The door opened to a dark passageway, which were exaggerated by the room's small confines. Jordan skimmed her flashlight across the walls, finding nothing but mold growing on drenched walls until the beam of the flashlight fell back into a protruded hall that opened up off the far back wall. Jordan tilted her head, trying to look down the partially concealed hall. A line of doors was strung down either end before it led into a dead end. She scanned the room one last time for any surprises and, with a deep breath, grabbed and her nose and gracelessly stepped inside.

A sticky musk festered in the room, discoloring the walls and calling the integrity of the floor below into question. Jordan took each step carefully, as if it would help, and carefully edged her way across the floor. She checked a swinging door, the first door on her left, and shined her flashlight around an industrial-sized kitchen. Broad-surfaced, stainless steel stretched across the edges of the kitchen, leaving gaps in ends and centers for stoves and a refrigerator that had been taken out or were never there to begin with. Two deep sinks were integrated into the far right counter. The farthest sink led down into a busted pipe that, at one time, had spewed water continuously across the floor, fostering the growth of mold and mildew between the cracks of the generic, white tile. The floor drains, designed to prevent flooding, instead collected puddles of water above their clogged holes. Jordan flinched at the idea of entering the kitchen and proceeded down the hall.

After the kitchen, Jordan found small clusters of rooms— each containing two bedrooms surrounding a pitiful bathroom and all left, like most of the rest of the house, completely bare. In comparison to the bedrooms elsewhere in the house, these were comparably small—only half the size of every other room she'd encountered. She found three sets of these bedrooms before reaching the hall's end, and their total area was just enough to fill in the massive gap on Jordan's map. A diminutive door stood at the end of the hall, and although Jordan figured it was a broom closet, she opened it just to check.

To her surprise, there were actually brooms inside, along with a heap of other cleaning supplies. She looked around in awe at the little artifacts left behind or probably forgotten. Then out of the corner of her eye, she saw a rack of hanging keys tucked away near the doorway. Jordan couldn't help but let out a squeal of excitement. She tore down the rack of fifty or so keys and carried them away and outside the rotted halls. Once she' cleared out of the darkened quarters, she set the rack of keys down, gawking in excitement at the fact that each key was labeled as to which door it opened.

Jordan sat down with the rack of keys in front and her map in hand, constantly glancing back and forth between the two, figuring out which keys she needed and which she didn't. Little scribbles by doors represented numbers and keyholes, and fortunately, she seemed to have all the keys to access the rest of the home.

Assuming there was probably nothing else in the flooded section she'd just left, Jordan scanned her map, looking for the most notable room she hadn't previously been able to check.

All the rooms in the center column proved to be monotonous, sharing identical furniture if any at all, and the only few worth noting were in the eastern most part of the upper west wing, the one room that was detached from the monotonous column.

The short corridor that diverged from the main hall in the upper west wing ended as a stunted hall, with only one door in its center facing outward. The faint imprint of the number *203* remained in the center of the door. Jordan shuffled carefully along sullied, rosewood floor. She pulled the keys, which she'd arranged on a carabineer for convenience, out of her pocket and shifted through them until she found number 203. She readied the key with a dubious sigh, and to her surprise, the key glided in effortlessly.

She fidgeted with the lock for a moment before the satisfying *click* of the lock let the door give way. The room, previously harbored and locked away, was a massive expanse of space. Light flooded through two grand windows whose design was similar to those in the main hall, filtered slightly by the thin, white, lace curtains that barely covered their broad surface. Snuggly betwixt the two grand windows, a king-sized bed had been carefully placed so that it was not under the window's direct light, and next to the bed, lined up against the right wall, was a dresser and a small vanity. Jordan crept forward into the room, swiveling her head and mindlessly glancing around the expanse.

She veered off toward the right side of the bed and saw a leather rucksack leaning against the bed as if it had been tossed there. Jordan stared quizzically at the out-of-place item, unable to think of why it would be there, before she took a few cautious step toward it.

She dug through to find that it had belonged to a soldier. Inside were a couple sets of old army work uniforms and one dress uniform. And after digging through the myriad of pockets, she looked at the equipment she'd found—a knife, a canteen, a fold-out spork, and a flashlight—along with, just as she had hoped, dog tags.

Curtis
David
RH Positive
Catholic

Jordan stared confused at the dog tags, wondering how this all tied into the house's history. She lay down on the bed, which resisted with a creaking squeak from the springs, and stared up at the ceiling with the tags in her hand.

CHAPTER 15

Travesties

Jessica stood hidden behind the open door, listening, listening to her husband's betrayal. She closed her eyes, taken by the dreadful sounds of her husband smothering his affection on another woman. This wasn't the first time this had happened, and Lord knew it wouldn't be the last. Jessica had been married to David now for eight years, and for the past two, David had begun to openly reject Jessica for another woman. Defeated, she sank to the floor listening to the perpetuation of her resentment and her overbearing feeling of being powerless in it all.

Her husband used to love her.

The first time such an incident had happened, she had been devastated. To her, it had been a sudden, desultory action that had instantly condemned the sanctity of their marriage.

But she could learn to forgive and forget one harmless affair because she knew her husband loved her and she couldn't imagine a life without him. Forgiving twice was just as easy as once had been, and Jessica learned to continue to forgive her husband's constant treachery. But she could never understand why she forgave the disdainful action. She coped through the anger, confusion, and depression. And caught in all of this emotion, she secluded herself in her peril, choosing a solitary silence that divided her from her family and friends. She could never define why she continued the deplorable act of forgiving the damning of their marriage, even when the one person she had dedicated her life to now seemed to never want anything to do with her. The fulfillment of her undesired curiosity about her husband's adultery became too much, and she lifted herself from the floor to escape the overbearing noise.

She wandered alone down the grand halls of her father's home. The estate of her now deceased father had been left to Jack, Robert, and David. She took a moment to look out the window to try and clear her mind. She tried to drown out malicious thoughts about her husband and his mistress with reassuring delusions of hope that even she knew weren't true—hopes of that, one day, David would renounce his narcissism and debauchery. She was simply trying to find some sort of possible prospect in this bleak marriage.

"Hey, Jessica," a friendly voice spoke out behind her. Jack entered a light jog to try and catch up with his sister.

"Hey, Jack," she muttered, too focused on counting floor tiles to pay attention to her brother.

"Everything okay?" he asked, knowing nothing was.

"Of course!" She perked up, looking her brother in the eyes.

Jack gave her an uneasy smile. He and everyone else in the house knew about the affair.

"Everything okay with you?" Jessica asked.

"Oh yeah!" Jack replied. "You know, business as usual."

"How is business going?" Jessica asked hesitantly.

"What can I say, business as usual," he replied, replicating the same eager tone to the same answer.

"I know—it's just that I've heard otherwise…" she began.

"Who told you that?" he inquired, insulted by such a bold claim.

"David," Jessica nervously replied.

Jack rolled his eyes and gave Jessica a perturbed look that questioned her husband's perspective.

"You know how David can exaggerate things," she added.

"Yeah, which is why you *really* shouldn't listen to him when he talks about things he doesn't know about."

"Yeah, but … he is my husband, and I should be able to trust him."

"You should …" Jack added dubiously. "I'll see you around dinnertime. I need to go check on some things in my office, and I'll be right there!" Jack slipped away into a branching hallway.

Jessica shook her head at her brother as he walked away. She had seen the numbers, and even she knew his bonds weren't doing well. But Jack always took the opportunity to discredit and slander David, regardless of whether Jack was actually at fault.

Jack's recent return from England just two years ago with a wife and three kids had interrupted everyone else's way of life at North Haven, particularly David's. David had reigned as the one man of the house, making all the judgment calls for the home, with Robert intentionally fading into the background of it all.

When Jack came back with an imperious attitude of control of the house, David naturally fought back. Their battle had endured for the next two years, as the two heads of the home fought each other every step of the way.

Dinner arrived every day as a constant challenge. Masses of bodies consisting of two families and one lone man shuffled around a fifteen-foot table trying to make their way to the same spot they sat in every night before. Five maids would cook and prepare one meal all night for both households and for the maids' own personal families.

Jessica watched carefully as her children were being served by their nanny, secretly criticizing everything she did. She was embittered by not knowing why David trusted the kids to that woman more than to their own mother. And despite her constant pleading with David to let her watch the kids, David always insisted.

"Now, Jessica, Judith is great with the kids. It's what she is trained to do and I just don't think you're cut out for raising them properly. Now would you quit being jealous and get over it?" He said this so apathetically and insisted that his mistress was a better mother.

As the chaotic shuffling diminished and everyone found his or her place around the table, a parade of food swept through the dining room door carried in on the arms of servants flooding out of the kitchen. Servants pushed carts and perfunctorily served each individual with the highest level of hospitality but in the most apathetic manner. Only Robert, Jessica, and her children ever bothered to thank them. And the children only did so to avoid a scolding glare from their mother.

Food prepared for hours worthy of any king was not spared a second thought, for as spectacular as it was, it was only a typical night for the family. As it did at the beginning of every joint meal, an awkward moment lingered over the table, everyone waiting for a sign it was okay to begin eating, for whoever would be bold enough to take the first bite. This was broken with David ravaging his carefully prepared steak with quick, brutal strokes of his knife. He never was a very composed diner. Everyone else at the table followed his lead, though at a more subtle approach.

The long, mahogany table was surrounded by the eleven who were the descendants of the original home owner or spouses of the descendants, along with two lesser guests, nannies who were only there to help the children. David sat at the head, with Jessica to his left and Jack at his right, both sitting perpendicular to David. Jack's wife, Violet, sat next to him and Pearl next to her. Robert was across from Violet and next to Jessica. At the end of the table were all the children. Jack had three—five-year-old Michael; four-year-old Jeffery, the middle son; and two-year-old Sally. The latter two were under the strict supervision of Nanny Ellice, who was always quick to silence the inappropriate outbursts of children. Across from Jack's kids were Jessica's two, Henry and Rachael. The former was six, the latter eight, and both were being watched by the young and beautiful Judith.

Dinner always found good company with the same banal questions of "How was your day?" This was usually followed by an equally boring answer of "Good." However, David was unusually boastful on days he'd returned from any sort of business trip.

"So how was the trip?" Jessica asked David, boring herself with her own question as she played with a bite of steak on her plate.

"Oh, it went great!" David began. "We put up five more wells, and all five are producing more oil than we expected. "He spoke with a gruff, deep tone and a mild southern accent, though the drawl of his vowels had been diluted by his time up east.

"I thought you said you had maxed out the number of wells on your property?" Jack asked a skeptically.

"Well, Jack, we've hired some new engineers who've managed to maximize the number of wells per acre."

"How are they managing that?" Jack grilled.

"If you must know, Jack," David answered scornfully. "We're able to take oil from surrounding fields by drilling at an angle," David said, holding his hand downward mimicking the angle.

"What? You're telling me is that you're stealing from your neighbors," Jack pointed out.

"Nonsense! I'm just looking out for my own enterprise. If my 'neighbors' choose to neglect the opportunities below them, that's their choice. But I won't let their 'ownership' deter me from using what they choose not to use," David rebutted. "Since you're so focused on disgracing my work, Jack, please tell me, how's your work is coming along?"

"It's going well," Jack replied timidly.

"Really?" David replied, sounding genuinely surprised. "Because I just saw that your investments just lost several thousand dollars," he added, discrediting his previous surprise. "Come on, Jack, son of one of the greatest stockbroker of the twentieth century and you're losing money? You should've really gotten into the oil business. The money just explodes out of the ground," David continued smiling haughtily, his tone laced with insult and pity.

No one dared interrupt their ritualistic squabble as the heads of household. And everyone else at the table only stared, eyes following the back-and-forth "banter" that continuously interrupted their meals. Usually, the two men of the house simply avoided eye contact and interaction and kept their separate ways. But when an interaction did take place between the two, it would end in a bellowing clamor that annulled any silence that had lingered in that emptiest of palaces.

"And be a thief like you? You steal from your neighbors," Jack yelled. "You take advantage of your business partners, swindling their money and time." Jack was now yelling, waving his finger and pointing as he presented each piece of evidence against his brother-in-law.

"Jack, you don't understand," David continued. Though his tone remained haughty, his voice was calm, passively shaming Jack's bouts and fits. "I'm only taking what I need to provide for our wonderful home—the one your father entrusted me with." This was something he liked to continually point out.

"He entrusted *us* with," Jack added with a bitter highlight on the word *us*.

"Maybe you'd like to pay for half of what it takes to keep this place running."

Jack sulked back, overcome with a mortifying silence. David smirked to himself and turned so as to no longer be confronting his brother-in-law. He chuckled to himself, pleased with his clear domination.

"Cheers, though," Robert raised his wine glass, "to our home, family and business."

The others meekly followed, with Jack hesitantly joining in the gratifying toast intentioned with ridicule.

Dinner ended with the perpetuating, somber silence that followed the toast. Jack quietly excused himself from the table, leaving in a condemned, embarrassed shuffle with Jessica glaring at David behind Jack's back.

"What? What'd I do?" David sneered, incredulous and exasperated by the tacit judgment.

Jessica withdrew her judging glare and dully looked back down to her plate to avoid his returned glare.

"Listen, I know I can be a little rough around the edges, but when you're jabbing yourself against me, don't expect yourself not to get hurt. Jesus, Jess, you of all people should know this. And when he's being a little, condescending prick all the time, I'm not just going to accept it."

"I know, but *just* try to be nicer to Jack, okay?" Jessica asked, hating herself for every submissive suggestion that should have been a demand.

David rolled his eyes apathetically and finished scraping off whatever was left on his plate.

Jessica shook her head, conceding to the truth of what was between them. It was hard not to doubt the meaning of their marriage when it could easily be abridged to his negligence and her eager acceptance of it.

The evening concluded with its traditional ending. Jessica tucked each of her kids into bed separately and wished them both a goodnight. She walked the halls of North Haven, heading to the same restful place she had just wished for her children. But ravaged and overcome by doubt and too disgusted by her husband to sleep by him, she wandered the empty halls. What he had done right after he'd gotten home from his trip and the way he'd treated Jack at dinner and every other action leading up to now left her thinking only of leaving him. For so long now, she'd wanted to finally leave her husband, but she never could truly imagine leaving it all behind. Twisted behind all his wrongdoing were the few rarities of goodness, which she appreciated more for their sparseness. Looking back now, even those few remarkable gestures had become less frequent and precious.

She still loved her husband, and she could never leave that behind. She remembered the man she'd met in her youth—the man who convinced her that he could sway the world with his charm but only for the good of society. She remembered a man who would sneak off and escape with her into the night away from North Haven's parties, who'd compelled her to believe nothing could be more than him. On their wedding day, Jessica had vowed herself to him unconditionally, and she had faithfully kept herself to that promise. She often thought of the challenges at hand as a crucible of her love and faith to her husband.

Down the hall, Jessica could see a faint glow sneaking out of the open door to Jack's office. She peered in to check on what her brother was doing this late and saw Jack hunched over, studying three logbooks all opened and arranged in a semicircle across his desk.

"What are you doing up this late?" she asked as she invited herself into the room.

"Just working," Jack replied unfazed, the greater part of his attention focused on his work and the rest to his sister, who he didn't even spare a glance.

"Is this about what David said?" she asked, knowing the answer.

With a heavy sigh, Jack stopped shuffling through the stock reports. "Yeah," he grudgingly admitted. "When he pointed out how much of a failure I've been in my career and that I couldn't afford to take care of my family, I felt like I was failing Dad," Jack muttered, hesitating between each clause.

"I'm sorry your career isn't taking off the way you planned, but you're just getting started. Don't feel like your life depends on making money." Jessica stepped into the room, comforting her stressed brother with a hand on his shoulder. "You're just new to it, that's all, and you'll get better! And I know David can be an ass—"

He scoffed before she could finish at the overt comment.

"But he loves you and you're family, and sometimes he and you forget that."

"I don't believe that," Jack replied.

"Believe it or not but you should hear the truth. And maybe if you were to have some faith in him, he might have some in you," Jessica stated, reassuring herself and Jack of her husband's forthrightness.

Jack pretended to ignore his sister, continuing to stare into the wall in front of his desk. Jessica walked out of the room, leaving Jack alone credulously teetering on an inadvertent lie.

Jessica continued, just as she had before, digressing to Jack's stubbornness. Reflecting on how fixable Jack's narrow-minded problems were, she returned to her own crucible. Waiting it out had only ravaged the past two years of her life with the deceitful hope of a promising tomorrow. Every time she pondered what to do, only one solution presented itself; it seemed that she would have to confront David about his faithless actions. But a nagging question always followed her bold thinking: What if he leaves?

"Oh, Lord, why does everything always have to be like this?" she said softly to herself. "I just want my husband back ... Maybe this *will* pass," she whispered, trying to reassure herself.

She shook her head knowing that she had told herself exactly that through the past two years. "It" had not yet and passed, and Jessica was utterly exhausted from her struggle to cope with the inexcusable fact of what her husband was doing. She wanted to leave him, knowing that it was ultimately the right solution and a righteous punishment for what he had done. But, as always, this thought was swiftly drowned by an undertow of emotion and memories that persuaded her she could not allow herself to abandon her husband because, ultimately, she loved him. She sighed; the frustration of her love, now compunction, weighed by the burden of needing to choose between possibly losing him or being neglected for the rest of her life, overcame her.

Awkward moments of disconnection and embarrassment followed the coming weeks as Jessica tried to cope with her inability to choose. Careful where she walked, Jessica would slip away into a nearby hall or door or whatever escape she found as subtly as she could if she heard so much as her husband's whisper. When David caught on and eventually exposed her with a quizzical look, her attempt at innocence was underscored by stutters and confusion.

"Jessica, is there something wrong? Have you been avoiding me?" David asked inquisitively, almost annoyed by his wife's apathy.

"I'm … fine, and no, why would you think that?" She responded with a smile, cringing at her own lie. The truth, on the brink of coming out, was held back only by her fear of losing her husband.

"You sure don't act 'fine,'" he responded, shrugging his shoulders, annoyed that he'd even bothered asking, and walked away.

She withdrew herself for the moment and forced herself to fester in the pain of her strife. She couldn't do this forever. She constantly balanced an internal battle—restraining her instinct, which despised both herself and her husband for everything he'd done; ignoring her incessant pleas for forgiveness from herself for still loving him. And, between the two, she succumbed under the pressure and forced into frustrating indecision. Ther choice was always too much for her to make alone.

Asking for help had always been a known obvious solution to her problem except for no one could undertsand. She knew what

Jack would say, her mother was completely oblivious to the issue, and what could Robert say that would be of any help? She shook her head because she had come to the same frustrating resoulition that had troubled her for the last two years. The most she could do is talk to someone, Robert.

After Eugene had died, Robert had become even more reclusive, always wandering the halls, taking walks around the grounds, or completely absent—"being unproductive," as David and Jack would always put it. She looked in the obvious places first. She checked his vacant room and his unused office and, from a window, scanned the lawn to see only the uninhabited, serene scape of North Haven's lawn. Jessica stood at the window a little longer, admiring the view and enjoying the carefree moment, until a thundering roll of children's feet darted down the hall behind her.

Jessica turned to look at the little interruption, as Jeffery chased Henry down the long stretch of the hall. Jessica, surprised, grew wide-eyed as the kids tore dangerously and, most importantly, carelessly down the hall.

"Henry! Jeffery! What do you think you're doing?" Jessica yelled at the oncoming bent of destruction.

Henry and Jeff immediately stopped on top of each other, almost skidding across the floor as they tried to brake their momentum.

With a domineering look that read as doom for the kids and their fun, she said sternly, "You know how dangerous it is to be running down the hall like that."

"Sorry, Mom," Henry replied solemnly.

"Yeah, sorry, Aunt Jessica; we won't ever do it again," Jeffery added, his own solemnity undermined by his devious smile.

"That's what you said last time, Jeffery."

"I know, but this time we promise we won't do it again!" Jeffery countered.

Jessica shook her head. "All right, but I just don't want you two tripping and getting hurt," she said. "Just don't run inside."

"We know, Mom," Henry said. "C'mon, Jeff, let's go " he added, continuing down the hall at a pace that suggested he was ready to take off running again.

Jessica shook her head, regretting that she hadn't punished the boys.

"Hey, have you guys seen your Uncle Robert?" she yelled down the hall to the two escaping kids.

"Uh, I think I saw him in the theatre," Jeffery answered, turning around dramatically while still walking backward.

"You mean the theatre you're not supposed to be in?"

"Uhhh, yeah, but …" Jeff looked for an excuse. "Rachael was there too, though!"

Jessica just rolled her eyes at the two deviants. What she wasn't sure of was what Robert would be doing in the auditorium. But given that it was her only lead, she headed down to the forgotten auditorium.

The auditorium, one of the greatest promises of North Haven, was now a forgotten closet for dust and silence. No one ever bothered with the auditorium and sometimes even Jessica would forget it existed as she passed by it on a daily basis. Jessica opened the double doors to a haunting silence disturbed by the creaking of the neglected door. With the home's initial legion of servants dwindled down to just five, many unnecessary parts of the home were left to be covered by dust. The mauling darkness that receded back into the empty chasm called into question whether anyone was actually here. Jessica patted the wall looking for a light switch and, with a lucky guess, found one and lit the forgotten room.

A harsh buzz from the light droned out the silence as the overhanging lights lit the massive room. No sound or sign suggested that anyone was in here, and she wondered if the children were just fibbing. But she continued looking around, wondering why Robert would be in here.

She hopped onto the stage and peered around behind the curtains, but nothing was there. She shrugged her shoulders and headed for the stage ledge. She was about to step down when she heard her daughter's giggling echoing from even further behind the stage. Jessica stopped to listen to the faint sound of her daughter's laughter.

"Rachael?" Jessica inquired, directing her question to the concealed stage, which responded with silence. But the laughter continued.

Jessica walked further down the stage, tracing the laughter back to a faint glow coming from a service room. The laughter was drawn out by a scintillating whisper. Jessica looked past the corner to see her daughter taken by awe as Robert drew the white outline of a cat drawn across the concrete wall.

"You see, you gotta go down with the curve, like this!" Robert said, standing off to the side of the drawing so Rachael could see.

Rachael tried to mimic his style, but her line deviated unnaturally, forming a hunch-shaped back. "See! I'll never be as good as you!" Rachael spat out in frustration.

"You just need to practice. You will always be worse the first time around, but if you give up now, all your cats will have poor, crooked backs."

Robert omnisciently looked behind him, knowing Jessica was watching. "Hey, Jess, I was just showing Rachael how to draw," Robert said, answering the question posed by the confused look on her face.

"In the storage room?" Jessica pointed out.

"Yeah, well … She kind of followed me here."

"Yeah!" Rachael interjected. "Did you know Uncle Robert has a piano in here?"

"He does?" Jessica asked, intrigued.

"Yeah! I followed him in here to see what he was doing!"

"Well … yeah," Robert admitted.

"So how'd you two end up drawing?" Jessica asked, now looking at the concrete wall marked with white chalk. Pairs of smiling faces randomly associated themselves next to cats and elephants, in pairs, one by an experienced drawer juxtaposed with the inexperienced student.

"Well, Rachael was following me because she wanted to learn and thought I could draw pretty well, so I found some marking chalk and showed her what I knew," Robert answered while looking at Rachael with a smile.

"Hey, Rachael, could you give me and Robert a moment alone?" Jessica asked.

"All right," Rachael muttered, wandering off into the hall.

"Is everything alright?" Robert asked, his questioning look adding to the concerned tone of his voice.

"It's been hard for me." She began, still hesitating to admit." ... Dealing with David." She still avoided the mention of the unspeakable.

"What about David?" Robert asked, sounding agitated about the topic.

"I just don't know how I can be with him any longer."

"Then don't. I mean, shouldn't it be obvious?" Robert spat.

She'd hoped Robert would have been more reasonable. "Never mind," Jessica remarked.

"What don't I understand?" Robert inquired incredulously.

"Forget I mentioned it," Jessica retracted, omitting what she thought to be a foolish truth.

"No, tell me. I want to know," Robert persisted.

"I don't want to say it. It sounds ridiculous."

"I want to help you, but I can't if you continue to hide from me and the rest of your family. Tell me how you feel," he insisted.

Jessica lingered on what he'd said, denying what she knew to be true—that her solitude had been self-inflicted, the result of omission and disconnection, rather than facing the issue that tormented her. She had pined away, choosing to wallow in negligence only hoping for the best.

"Robert, the truth is ..." She faltered. "I still love David," Jessica confessed, feeling foolish for stating the obvious.

Robert paused for a moment in thought, halted by the simple statement.

"I still love him for all the great things that he once did for me, and I just think you've only seen the bad in him."

"Well," Robert began with a look of understanding. He turned away, hiding a sudden paleness that took him by surprise. "No, I do know," He began "The moment I had failed to commit myself to…a person I loved was the moment I lost that person. I would never again give a halfhearted effort for someone I love." Robert remarked fervently.

"You're right … I guess maybe I was hoping you'd say something different." Jessica paused. "But what if he chooses differently?"

Robert sighed as the pinnacle of his passion died down into simple words. "I suppose that's the risk you have to take."

Jessica stared back at Robert with dread, ultimately facing the unpleasant solution that was her only option. "I guess I'll just have to do it then … later." Jessica's remark.

Robert turned to Jessica with a startled, firm look. "No! You must do it soon! Tonight!" Robert said fervently.

Jessica cringed. "I don't know if I can do that, Robert."

"I know it won't be easy, but if you don't do it soon—if you don't do it tonight—you'll regret it. I did,"

Jessica turned away from her brother with a lot to think over. "She shook her head, lost in the vision of the moment when she would need to confront her husband—to ask the embarrassing question of whether he still loved her. The conflicting vision of herself making the same mistake she'd made for the past two years arose as a taunting challenge. She needed to confront her husband. The notion alone was intimidating; the details obscure.

For right now it remained a distance, comfortable unformed thought.

*   *   *

The evening lazily carried on with the routine family dinner. Everyone was called in from his or her corner of the home to come together for less than an hour for dinner. Jessica hid in plain sight behind an unbearable silence of anxiety and dread. She perched over in her chair, staring blankly at her plate, trying to formulate just what to say to him.

David, I think we need to rethink our relationship. She pondered. *No, too vague. David, I want to be the only girl in your life.* She stopped herself. *Too nice.*

David, I'm leaving you. She paused, terrified by the possibility alone.

She shook her head, not even sure of when to even say whatever she would say. She glanced over at David, far off at the head of the table, ignoring everything besides his plate. She would do it after dinner, when they were alone.

Dinner concluded as the family members individually left until only David, Jessica, and Violet and her children were left sitting. David gracelessly finished his dinner with a last shoveling of whatever food was on his plate and finished up with an exaggerated stretch.

"That was good, James," he remarked hollowly to his butler, who stood to the right of him, as he excused himself from the table. He walked out of the dining room with Jessica trailing from behind.

As she peered around the corner David rounded, she immediately stopped. The seemingly distant David stood right in front of her, glaring down at her with a peeved look.

"Jessica, why are you following me?" David queried.

"I, uhh, I'm not following you. I was just headed up stairs," she stammered, nervously gesturing toward the stairs.

"God, you're weird," he commented incredulously, walking away. Jessica wanted to shout, "Wait." But she didn't know what to say after that. She shook her head in discouragement, trying to convince herself that, next time, she would do it. She caught a glimpse of Judith joining David as he continued down the hall and knew she had to do it now.

CHAPTER 16

Unconditional

Nighttime left just the few essential, lingering lights scattered randomly through the home to the few people who were awake. David escaped to a far-off guest room at the edge of the home but beyond anyone's attention. He sat at the edge of a small table, facing an empty chair with a half-empty bottle of whiskey and stared at the shadowed doorway with a promiscuous grin. With a slow creak, the door came ajar, the figure beyond it hidden from view in the dark room and then came a slow, subtle shuffling of footsteps.

"Hey, I've been waiting for *you* all night," David slurred toward the half-lit figure.

"Well sorry to keep you waiting," an enchanting voice responded from the dark. Judith stepped out of the concealing shadow, striding up to David, who just looked up at her with a lewd look.

"You know, maybe we shouldn't make it so obvious where we meet," David joked, his sense of humor exaggerated by the last few shots of whiskey.

"Well, maybe if you would just split with that wife of yours, we wouldn't have to worry about all this," Judith snorted, leaning over the table, closer to David.

"Just leave her out of this." David rolled his eyes at her incessant suggestions.

"Oh, come on, David, you know feel the same way. I don't know why you stick around here with her. I bet you don't even love her anymore!" Judith protested as David just shook his head in ridicule.

David subtly chuckled at himself in another predicament with Judith. What was he going to do with her? "Maybe I just keep her around to remind me of how sweet you are," he remarked cleverly, trying to save the situation.

"Oh, David!" Judith replied as she sat carefully on David's lap, hanging herself around his shoulders. Judith caressed his neck and slowly kissed David.

A unwelcome watcher waited in the dark, shadowed doorway, unnoticed by the philanderers. The voyeur took a step forward, creeping close enough to see but staying far enough back to remain unseen. A prolonged groan from the disturbed floorboard announced the intruder, stopping David midkiss.

He looked past Judith. "Who's there?" he snarled out to the darkness.

The figure slowly walked out. Jessica stood at the fringes of the visible light. She stood paralyzed with a shaken look on her face, slowly walking to finally try and confront David.

"Jessica, what are you doing here?!" he yelled.

"David," she stuttered, fighting the fear that quickly overwhelmed the courage she had finally mustered to end their marriage. "I really don't think you value our marriage!"

"Jessica, not now!" David yelled, pushing Judith off his lap to stand.

"No, David, we need to talk about this now!" Jessica demanded.

"Fine! You want to talk about *our marriage*? Let's go!" He stomped over and grabbed Jessica by the arm, leading her out to the hall.

"Let go of me!" Jessica wailed, violently pulling her arm away from David's grasp.

"Jessica, I just want to talk to you about *our marriage*," David said patronizingly, in a feigned, mocking sympathetic tone.

"David, why are you acting like this? You've never been this way!" Jessica shouted.

"I don't know, Jessica! Maybe it's because you barged in here during *my* quiet time wanting to talk about something ridiculous!"

"Our marriage is not ridiculous!" Jessica interrupted, biting her lip, trying to fight back the tears that hung on the brim of her eyes.

"No, but it is ridiculous that you would openly question it," David retorted, openly ignoring that Judith was still standing behind him.

"David, do you think I'm stupid? I know why you're here with Judith!" Jessica snapped, pointing a jagged, incriminating finger at Judith, who stood in silent awe in the back corner of the room.

"What do you think I'm doing with Judith?" David opened his arms in dissent, openly dancing around the true reason she was here.

"I know you're sleeping with her, and everyone knows! David, I can't be married to a man who doesn't respect me or our marriage."

David recoiled from such an assumption, wide-eyed and shaken, and stumbled for a moment, looking for the words that would save himself. "I can't believe you would accuse me of that! You're my wife, and I would expect that you, of all people, would trust me!" David shouted.

"David, I can't do this anymore!"

"Do what anymore?" he spat out incredulously.

"I can't be with a man who neglects me and lies to me. You've destroyed everything we've put into this and although I will always love you, I can't stand being with you anymore!"

"What the hell are you saying, Jessica?"

"You heard me! It was you who ruined this and you who is forcing me to walk away from it! It's been all your fault!"

"Oh my God, just shut up!" David roared as he slapped Jessica across the face, knocking her to the floor in a loud thud of shaken floorboards and ended peace. David recoiled from the slap, panting with frustration, until he noticed Jessica's limp body lying motionless on the ground.

He lurched over her body. Behind him, Judith screamed profane, incomprehensible things at him. And as he realized what he'd done, he backed away in disbelief and darted for the door at the far edge of the room.

David scuttled down the hall and down the steps to the side entrance of the home. As he made his escape to the side foyer, he passed Jack heading in the opposite direction.

"What was that noise?" Jack asked curiously.

"What noise?!" David responded, offended by the question. He continued past Jack.

"Where are you going?" Jack shouted to David, who was already halfway down the hall.

David didn't reply and just continued to his escape. He threw open the doorway carelessly, leaving the it open, and fled to the garage. He jammed his keys into the ignition, and just as he was ready to drive off, he stopped himself for a moment of reflection. He listened to the chirping of the crickets cutting through the calm, silent summer night before driving off and away from his uncorrectable mistake.

CHAPTER 17

Escape from North Haven

D avid was crouched down in the crowded landing craft, weighed down by his oversized knapsack, soaked clothes and a hangover from the night before. He was drenched from the incessant splashing of seawater and packed into the boat with about forty other men from the Fourth Infantry Division, all of whom were suffering the same fate. They had been drifting at sea for the past forty-five minutes, waiting for a naval escort to guide them ashore. Aside from the inane, subtle complaints of a few men, the entire platoon remained unnaturally quiet, preferring to somberly look out at the foggy horizon in expectation of some imminent doom waiting for them ashore. David himself was pretty shaken by the whole ordeal. It was only a few days ago that command had revealed the purpose of the past year's training—constant drills of landing procedures and equipment briefing for a landing mission. They were headed for the beaches of Normandy. David stared off in the general direction the landing craft, imagining the worst waiting for him on the shore. The past two years of training had cumulated into the stress and panic of this one day, and he was waiting for it all to happen.

David continued to stare off into the fog for a few minutes more before he noticed the radioman breaking the monotony and shuffling through the other men to tell the platoon commander something. David watched him move up, hoping for some news soon.

"Do you think we might be moving soon?" David whispered to the closest soldier.

The soldier turned to look at David, but David couldn't recognize him. "I hope so. I can't stand this." he replied.

"I know. Me too," David added in solidarity.

The drifting boat's engine abruptly cranked up, and the boat's unintentional drift became an intended, rough glide following other landing crafts headed in the same direction. Heads turned in question and looked at each other asking about the sudden change.

"Listen up!" the silhouette of Sergeant Thatcher yelled from the bow of the boat. "The PT escort arrived, and we should be debarking in about five minutes!"

David could recognize that scratchy, disgruntled voice anywhere. He straightened his crouch, bracing for whatever was coming within the next five minutes. He had accepted the dreadful fact of where he was going, but he never liked it. And worst of all, he had no idea what would happen.

As they approached the shore, bursts of gunfire, quick flashes, and loud cannonade came from the beachhead ahead towards their direction. Boats crashed across the entire side of the beach, as swarms of men charged out of them madly, running full speed into the uphill fog. David readied his rifle as the landing craft crookedly slammed into the shoreline. The hull door dropped down, and in the brief initial instance, forty men stared confused at the open door before their training guided them out of the craft.

David shuffled out to the hatched door and leaped into the frigid ocean, just as he had done in the countless drills. The tides of men who had come before him had already secured the beach, eliminating any danger. The few bunkers at the top of the hill had already been silenced by those who had arrived before him, anticlimactically leading to a victory David hadn't imagined nor deserved. Gunshots still rang in the distance, as David's platoon made it up the beachhead and gathered beside one of the German bunkers. The platoon looked confused and surprised by the unexpected victory.

"Form up on me!" Staff Sergeant Thatcher yelled in his scratchy, monotonous tone.

David turned and followed the invariably pissed-off sergeant. Thatcher must have been in his midforties. He had a wrinkled, worn face exaggerated by a full, shadeless white beard. During the rare moments when he wasn't shouting orders or chewing out some unlucky soldier, he was off talking with the lieutenant or smoking.

"All right, you see that smoke over there?"

The entire platoon looked behind them to see a billow of smoke just off the coast to their right.

"That's where we were supposed to land, and we need to double-time it over to those bunkers and clear them out. Word is that the Omaha Beach landing party is gettin' it, and we're going to clear out the bunkers givin' them a hard time."

"How in the hell did we end up over here?" some random soldier perked up and asked.

Thatcher let out a huge, exaggerated sigh. "You think I fuckin' know? I just do what the lieutenant tells me to do, and he doesn't even know how to put his pants on one leg at a time in the morning without my help! Anyone else have any stupid fuckin' questions?" He didn't allow them a second to make any. "All right, let's fall out." Thatcher waved his arms.

As the rest of the platoon followed his lead, David was caught along in the mess of it all.

The mile-long trek around the coastline to their intended landing spot nearly winded David as he was carrying a full knapsack. They encountered no resistance as they marched, save for the intimidating sounds of canon and machine gun fire that drowned out their footsteps in the sand. All around them, the cacophony of war rang out—the snare of cannon fire being met with the retaliatory rhythm of machine gun fire—but in their immediate proximity, there was no war.

The platoon came up to an unsuspecting group of bunkers facing the sea, and David followed the rest of his squad and took up a defensive position at a good, safe distance around the bunkers. The machine gun fire became unignorable now; every second was filled with its incessant clamor as fire hailed down at more incoming landing craft.

"Jurkowski! You're clear! Set up those chargers! Second Squad do the same!" Squad Sergeant Corbin barked, the order barely heard over the machine gun fire.

Immediately, a combat engineer scurried forward from behind David with a large wooden block hollowed out with TNT and a stick at the back to keep it upright. The engineer set it up at the back of the door before running back into cover.

"Charges set!" the engineer yelled in a scraggy voice.

Over the hill, a small hand with a thumbs-up popped out from behind a rock.

"Second Squad's good to go!"

"Clear!" the engineer bellowed.

David opened his mouth like they'd taught him in training, so the force of the explosion didn't rupture his ear. He covered his ears and turned away from the door in anticipation of the explosion but it never went off. He looked back at the motionless charge which gave no warning of its volatility. A distant thud went off from the bunker next door, and everyone looked over to his right to see Second Squad storm the blasted-off door. The machine gun fire out of First Squad's own bunker paused in response to the nearby explosion. David and the rest of First Squad looked back to their own charge, which remained unchanged.

"Well fuck," Corbin muttered.

"Now what? Do we knock?" some faceless soldier sneered.

"Shut up!" Corbin growled.

The squad stared down the motionless door from the safety of cover, expecting something to happen.

The engineer let out a sigh. "I'll go check out that charge," the engineer groaned.

"Good idea," Corbin affirmed condescendingly.

The engineer leaped from behind his rock once again and tiptoed toward the door, purposely avoiding its opening.

"Bunker two is clear!" a voice shouted from the other.

The engineer continued slowly to the precarious charge next to the threat. David quivered from the safety of his rock, carefully watching as if he was guiding the delicate movements of the brave engineer. A sudden pause interrupted the tense moment as a sudden, rusty creak turned everyone's attention toward the now slightly cracked door. David moved his head to the right, trying to see what was peering out but couldn't get a good angle. He aimed his rifle, but before he could fire, someone had already taken a snap shot at the door, which immediately shut again.

"Damn it! Who did that?" Sergeant Corbin asked with no response. "Well come on! Pick it up, Jurkowski!" Corbin sneered toward the engineer.

"Well … maybe they'll surrender," the engineer suggested.

"Yeah and I can't wait around for that day. Now come on; smoke their asses already!"

The engineer mumbled some curses before resuming his careful shuffle toward the bomb. He took a moment tinkering with the charge, swearing all the while, before hastily running back.

"Clear," he yelled bitterly, probably rolling his eyes.

David reopened his mouth, and this time, an overpowering shock wave swept over him, ringing his ears and rattling his whole body as the force of the directed explosion ruptured the bunker.

"First and Second Squad, move down and do a clean sweep on the beaches. Curtis and Sparkles will clear out the bunkers while Brenan covers them," Corbin ordered.

David had been heedlessly staring at the blasted bunker the entire time, thinking over what had happened. As his squad dispersed around him, David stood alone, looking at the remains of the indiscrete bunker.

"Curtis! What are you doing?" Corbin yelled as he glared at the confused soldier.

"Uh … I don't know, Sergeant."

Corbin rolled his eyes before meeting David's eyes with a hateful stare.

"Go clear out the bunker with Sparkles and Brenan," Korbin sneered at David, his tone hushed and careful, so no one could hear him but David.

"Yes, Sergeant!" David nervously leapt from behind his rock to try and make up lost time and scurried toward the bunker.

Two soldiers who were indistinguishable silhouettes outfitted in standard issue army uniforms—presumably Sparkles and Brenan—were walking toward the busted bunker door. David didn't really know the names of anyone in his platoon other than his sergeant's, the staff sergeant, and the second lieutenant. Before deployment, he had been told that he would be deploying with the unit he had trained with, but in a mad scramble before D-Day, administration had randomly assigned him to this unit to fill in a spot for an injured soldier.

"Are you done standing there with your head up your ass?" Brenan asked.

"Sorry, I just forgot where I was" David answered.

The three causally walked toward the bunker, ignoring the war around them.

"I'll cover you two," Brenan said as they approached the bunker.

Sparkles and David looked at each other and nodded in agreement, but David felt the awkward scorn of being a newcomer expecting trust.

Sparkles took the first step into the bunker with his rifle raised. He treaded through the dark confines of the bunker. David followed his lead, rifle raised, and mirrored Sparkle's movements. Five dead German soldiers lay tossed against the front walls of the bunker with the previously deafening machine gun knocked over and lying atop of the dead. David checked his side of the bunker. He saw a mess of large wooden splinters that he made out as what used to be a small, wooden table accompanied by a set of chairs buried underneath chunks of concrete and papers but no survivors.

"Clear," David said.

"Clear," Sparkles echoed.

The two exited the bunker, moving less cautiously then they had when they'd entered. And just before David left, he looked at one of the dead men, who lay catatonic but unscathed except for a few bloodied scratches on his face. His eyes belied his unharmed complexion. His pupils remained motionless, staring off in the direction of a wall but transfixed on an imperceptible oblivion that only the dead could see. It had been something that David had seen before he joined the army. He turned away, denying his curiosity.

David, Sparkles, and Brenan continued on and cleared the next bunker and met up with their appropriate squads, which had secured the beach for incoming landing craft. Countless landing craft randomly blotted the sea, converging on the shore. The squad stood speechless at the shoreline holding the beach as the second wave of reinforcements sailed in on landing craft, crashing in upon the shoreline. A droning buzz from the radio interrupted the climactic moment. The radioman waited for the end of the message before responding with a, "Yes staff, sergeant."

"We're rallying over at Thatcher's position along with the 101st Airborne," the radioman announced to the group.

"Then I guess we shouldn't be standing around. Let's move out," Corbin echoed, gesturing his hand toward inland.

David groaned at the thought of marching forward. His back hurt. His feet ached. And the thirty pounds of equipment he carried diminished his will. But with or without him, Corbin led the march as every soldier followed behind him, clustered together and strung out. David unwillingly trudged along behind them all. He looked down and sighed, finally realizing what he had gotten himself into, before looking to the sky in a release of frustration. And as the soldiers marched on, a cool breeze glided across the open grounds of the fields of Normandy. Blowing without interruption, it swept through the unorganized ranks of soldiers who marched indefinitely into the distant blue edge of the horizon.

CHAPTER 18

Unexpected Redemption

The weeks following the initial anticlimactic landing had remained anticlimactic. Since the initial landing, David and the rest of the Fourth had been assigned to a spot just a mile inland of their landing. They'd made makeshift camps around one of the nearby inland towns that the 101st Airborne had secured upon landing. The expected crucible of war that had kept David awake at night so far had devolved into unloading equipment from the incoming landing craft. A constant stream of packages and boxes came in, ranging from food to flame throwers—everything you would need to start a war. David had been working sixteen hours a day, performing the tedious labor of unloading and sorting through it all. He thought that he alone had unloaded enough equipment for every soldier to have at least one of everything. But somehow, command was still complaining about limited supplies. He tried not to complain, but he just hated the work. He'd spent the past two years of his life training to go to war, and now he was just unloading crates, which felt entirely against his purpose.

David had been unloading and unpacking rations all day with one of his squad mates Ben Larkin. He took a crowbar and pried off the side of the box to reveal unfathomable layers of cans, with the simple label, "BEEF," on each one. He was tasked with placing the cans in smaller metal containers for ease of transport, and just as he grabbed one of the containers Foster, one of his platoon mates, interrupted him.

"Hey we're doing a briefing, and they're lookin' for ya. Didn't anyone tell you?" Foster asked, panting from his run.

"No," David replied dubiously, now worried about getting into trouble.

"Well, what are ya doin' lookin' at me for? Let's go!" Foster said, motioning his thumb toward the deserted church that command used as a temporary headquarters.

"You're late," Staff Sergeant Thatcher commented, interrupting himself as David tried to slip in without being noticed, with Foster casually strolling in behind him.

The platoon was seated in the two rows of benches where a congregation would normally sit, with Thatcher up front acting as the preacher for the substitute congregation.

"I didn't know there was a meeting."

Thatcher let out a prolonged, exaggerated sigh that let David know it wasn't his fault. "Between you and these two, we're never gonna make it through the briefing. And we're still missing people! Foster, what the fuck you doin'? I still don't see Campbell or Morgan!"

"I'll get *right* on it, Sergeant," Foster responded as he left the church, leaving the door open behind him.

Thatcher resumed his sigh as Foster left. "Before I got interrupted," he started, staring and shaking his head at David, who sulked in the back corner, "I was saying that B and C Company are going to serve as the vanguard of the whole operation and will be liberating the town of Montebourg to get a forward position on our real target, Cherbourg." His gruff, angry voice carried easily in the church. "It should be left undefended with German forces all but cut off and retreating back into Cherbourg. B Company will move in through here." He gestured to a map of Normandy he had hung up at the front of the chapel. "And we're moving in through here along with the rest of C Company." As he pointed to the southwest road entering the town.

Thatcher continued for the next ten minutes, explaining the operation in minute detail. He laid out the positioning of every man and how things should go on an ideal battlefield. David never really cared for the details and just followed along in whatever direction the squad moved.

"We'll be given light mortar support before the assault, but it should be a pretty easy mission. So don't fuck it up!" Thatcher jeered as he glared back at David, who was still sulking in the corner.

Everyone else appreciated the joke with the best laugh they could manage before a war.

"Any questions?" Thatcher concluded.

"When's this happening?" David asked innocently, raising his hand from the back corner.

"Maybe you'd know if you hadn't been late for the meetin'," Thatcher replied, peeved. "It's happenin' on the twentieth,"

Thatcher added referring to his clipboard. "All right, if there's no questions, then get back to work."

A few soldiers left immediately, leaving the rest behind to comment among themselves. But gradually, every soldier began to get up, stretch, and shuffle.

"What about Campbell, Morgan, and Foster?" a random soldier asked, his identity hidden among the crowd of scrambled men.

"What about 'em? You think I or they care if they know what's goin' on? They can ask their squad sergeant, who did attend the meetin', if they care."

There was no rebuttal to Thatcher's response as all of C Company shuffled out of the deserted church and back to their post.

June 20th was only a couple of days away, proving that the army was very fond of its surprises. David was almost fond of this particular surprise too. The two nights before the mission proved to be just as restless as the nights before the landing had been, and knowing that the day of the mission was just around the corner relieved some of the anxiety of waiting. David had no idea what combat would actually be like, and just as he had been uneasy the few days before the landing, he was uneasy now. Countless training exercises had ostensibly prepared him for every conceivable combat scenario, but those sessions always excluded the real dangers. David wasn't sure how he would brave against actual bullet fire, and he spent those two nights attempting to rally himself to believe that he would be okay. Those two sleepless days were only a momentary sanctuary for him, and despite his efforts to cope with the upcoming day, the day of the mission, he wasn't ready by the time it came.

It had been an early, peaceful morning that had been suddenly interrupted by random gunshots and small flashes ahead in the town of Montebourg. Even farther off to the east, David caught the echo of tank fire roar across the field. Armored support was supposedly taking on a Panzer division, but David really knew nothing about that. He just marched quietly along with the rest of his company toward the unsuspecting town. It felt pretty stupid to be just marching out in the open like they were. David could only imagine that one good mortar barrage would take out the lot of them.

But to David's surprise, nothing fired on the squad as the men marched across the empty field, and regardless of his pessimism, C Company arrived at the town of Montebourg unscathed. The men reached a street that led up into the town with a large, brick wall covering their advance on the left side of the street. They crouched down, each in a defensive position. Sergeant Corbin signaled the squad toward the wall with a wave of his finger, and without hesitation, each squad member darted across the street, getting his backs as close to the wall as his knapsack would allow.

David looked around, trying to spot out any danger. Open and shut windows up above, concealing bushes and shrubbery, a picket fence covering a lawn—a collection of invaluable cover, all available for anyone to hide behind. There had been no immediate sense of danger, but the looming sense that his own demise was near lingered in every dark corner of this city. The sheer number of possibilities seemed to be what was really putting him on edge.

"I guess no one's home," one soldier remarked as the squad entered the town through one of the side roads that stretched along its border.

"They're home; they just don't want to come out and play," another added sarcastically. A few of the men laughed, and David shared a smile. The comment wasn't that funny, but it seemed to relieve some of the stress.

The men proceeded up the street to be immediately interrupted by the loud rattle of distant machine gun fire coming from their west. Everyone flinched at its sudden appearance. David had tucked his head under his rifle, trying to hide from the possibility of fire. And once everyone realized the fire had come from further down the block, they all stood up from their balk with a shared sigh of relief and a little laugh before continuing their slow ascent up the city streets at the pace of a crawl. The machine gun fire continued to intermittently clatter on, emphasizing the threat harbored in the desolate town.

"Anyone from C Company, do you copy?" a loud, omnipotent voice rang out from the back of the squad. Everyone turned to look at the radio man, who had been fidgeting with the dials on his radio pack.

"Turn that thing down, Scott!" Corbin quietly yelled from the front of the squad.

Corporal Scott raised an annoyed finger that asked for a second.

"This is Squad One of Second Platoon, C Company," Scott called back on the radio.

An anxious pause followed as the entire squad stared back with uncertainty, waiting for a radio response.

"Hey now, not all at once on the channel, I need support from at least one platoon to come and flank this German machine gun position. Third Platoon is completley held up on the main south road coming into the town. I thinks it's, uh … Rue Paul somethin'."

"Rue Paul somethin'," one soldier up front pondered out loud. "I sorta remember that place from the briefin'."

"Well where is the machine gun at?" Corbin asked Scott.

"Where's the machine gun at?" Scott repeated on the radio.

"It looks like it's on some sort of cafe balcony or somethin'. Just at an intersection," the voice over the radio responded.

"Everyone else hear that?" the radioman asked over the radio.

"Copy that. Third Squad is en route."

"First Squad is right behind ya guys!"

David looked back to see Third Squad just down the road from where they were.

"Let Thatcher know we're moving in," Korbin said to the radioman.

"Thatcher, you copy?" Scott asked into the radio before getting immediately interrupted.

"What the fuck's my name?!" a scratchy voice came over the speaker, dominating the radio channel.

"Correction, Sergeant Thatcher, Second Platoon is moving in to help Third, who look like they're held up somewhere close by. We're moving in to help."

"Understood. The cross street for Rue Paul is probably Rue du Maupas. Do you copy that, Squads One and Three? Rue Du Maupas!"

"Copy that!" the two squads confirmed.

David's squad continued up the road for another block or so before stopping at a street sign that read Rue du Maupas. The machine gun fire echoed further down, maybe a block or so by David's guess.

"What do we do, Sarge?" Sparkles asked Corbin, who was staring intensely down Rue du Maupas without any insight.

"I don't know, boys ... Let's just wait for good ol' Sergeant First Class Thatcher to lead the way."

"What the fuck's the holdup?" Sergeant Thatcher bellowed from behind them, enraged.

Third squad had managed to catch up to them, with Sergeant Thatcher leading them forward. David almost burst out laughing at Thatcher's nearly comical approach. He always managed to maintain a monotone voice that sounded permanently irritated.

"Whadda ya think, boss? Should we head down Maupas right here or keep going?" Corbin asked Thatcher.

Thatcher shook his head, followed by his signature sigh. Thatcher looked down the cross street of Rue de Maupas and then back down the street they were on. "This one doesn't look like it goes through another cross street for another few blocks, which means we'll have gone too far. But this street will put us right with B Company, which doesn't help anyone if were pinned up with 'em," Thatcher said, pondering the options out loud.

"Thanks, boss. I can think for myself. I just can't decide where to go."

"Oh Yeah!" Thatcher responded, almost dumbfounded. "Why don't ya think of where to go, ya clown?" He snapped with a dramatic eye roll. "Look though, this one is a nice funnel for us to die in with no cover on the street and countless positions in the window up above to shoot at us from. We're not going that way." Thatcher pointed. "We're going down Maupas," he concluded.

"You're the boss," Corbin muttered as he gestured his squad to take a left down the street.

David didn't really care what street they went down; both looked dreadfully long and precarious. Another eruption of gunfire coming from the left joined in with the repetitive machine gun fire and its retaliatory fire that came from the right of the squad.

"Squads Two and Four are under fire! I repeat, Squads Two and Four are under fire!" the radio blared. The transmission was interrupted by gunfire and shouting.

"Shit, I guess someone is home. Should we go back and help?" one soldier asked with a nearly panicked tone.

"Naw, if they needed help, they would've asked. I'm not worried about a couple of squads that can handle themselves when a full company is being held down." Thatcher replied.

The street ahead of them shared the same iconic design they'd encountered in the rest of city. David had seen the Tudor style architecture all over France before the war on his many trips here. And despite that the city was left destitute, it still reminded him of those trips he'd taken here with his wife and kids.

The two squads climbed over the stone fence that lined the front lawns of the row of houses parallel to the street for better cover. David looked up to the windows of the homes on both sides of the street, vigilantly watching before seeing a couple of shadows dart through the frame of a window.

"Anyone one see that?" David mumbled.

"What?" Larkin asked from behind him.

"Did you see that in the window?" David asked again, pointing like a lunatic up toward a random window.

"Nope," Larkin replied skeptically.

David fell back to just marching, trying to keep his head forward to avoid looking at the windows. He felt pretty foolish for openly pointing out easily disputable and questionable evidence. Despite his efforts, his mind wildly extrapolated what he'd just seen—a lurking shadow of a German sniper stalking their unit and waiting to take them all out one by one or maybe another machine gun team waiting to slaughter them all in the open. David looked back to the window, just to find some foolish solace in the vacancy. He maintained his stare, despite nothing being there.

"I swear I saw something," he muttered to himself. And just as he tried to reassure himself of his sanity, the figment of his imagination slid out from the cover of the window, holding a submachine gun.

"Shit! Get down!" someone yelled before he could as the empty sets of windows to the right of them suddenly filled with the town's occupants, ready to repel invaders.

A wild spray of cobblestone blocks rained down around David while he voluntarily crashed to the ground behind the cover of the fence. He saw his fallen squad mates fallen lying with him or crouching behind the fence under the torrent of incoming fire. Some of them looked like they'd fallen involuntarily, lost in their own actions just before being stopped by a bullet and sent splaying to the ground.

After the initial hail of fire, the submachine guns stopped, and only the intermittent cackle of rifle fire could be heard. The strike had happened so quickly, and David's fear convinced him he was dumbfounded as to what to do. Two weeks behind enemy line, and he had never been fired upon. And despite the forced, almost daily rifle drills during his life in the army in preparation for the day he would need to retaliate, his will to follow that training had been lost.

Squad Three, who had been about ten feet ahead of them before the firefight, was providing some supportive fire, with Sergeant Thatcher directing the squad's fire as he moved over toward David's squad. David cowered with his back against the cobblestone, nervously clenching his rifle as his squad mates around him either found the courage to retaliate or joined David in hiding. He fought the urge to flee, but his courage only managed to keep him hid behind the fence. And what David speculated to be the innumerable seemed to quickly die off as the harsh clink of the German's bolt-action rifles abruptly ended.

Sergeant Thatcher marched over toward David, still cowering behind the fence. He realized the rest of the squad was moving in to clear the building and got up to try and join the group.

"What the fuck were you doin'?" Thatcher yelled, his face flushed the red of a hot iron.

"Uh … I was … not unnecessarily throwing myself into dangerous circumstances, Sergeant!" David explained, paraphrasing the army handbook.

"I don't want to hear it, boy. And what were you hiding from? They weren't even firing at you," Sergeant Thatcher said, pointing to the two dead men ten feet away who looked as if they had just been knocked down from their heroic stance. One medic was attending them in a vain attempt to save their lives.

"Sorry, Sergeant, I guess I didn't know what was going on," David stuttered pitifully. He couldn't imagine anything to say that might lighten the situation. Sergeant Thatcher sighed almost showing a glimpse of empathy for David.

"Boy, what are you doing here?" Thatcher asked sedately, as if sunk by a sort of inner defeat.

"I'm here to fight a war, Sergeant!" David answered.

"Don't bullshit with me, boy. Why did you join the army?"

David stopped himself from answering, unable to find an understandable justification for why he was here. After a night of drinking, one appealing army poster featuring the blown-up words, "Follow me!" and a soldier charging to victory, leading the reader on with an open-handed wave of his arm. That poster had been more than enough, at the time, to recruit David. And he still couldn't figure out why. A year before that, he had left his family and his. He had been a successful businessman before he'd left, but after abandoning his family, he'd chosen to blow it all on luxury and alcohol. And after only a year of that, he just couldn't find any meaning to it. An army poster picturing a glorious moment of victory had seemed to offer everything he'd ever wanted.

"I guess I came here to escape," David finally concluded.

"A lot of these boys came here just to do that. That's what I wanted to do twenty years ago. Fresh out of school, I saw the army promising all the glory I could imagine, and at that age, that's all I ever wanted."

"I guess this isn't what I wanted. Sergeant Thatcher, is there any way I can go back now? I don't think I want to 'escape' anymore," David pleaded.

Thatcher solemnly shook his head.

"You're in the shit pot now, boy, and you'll learn to live in it. C'mon, enough chitchat; you'll stick with me, and I'll show you how to make it." Thatcher gestured with an open-handed wave for David to follow.

The two chased off after the squads that had gone before them, through the overcast streets of Montebourg.

CHAPTER 19

Reproach of a Father

Adventitious gunfire erupted in pockets across the town of Miesbach as the German defenders tried to brave the outnumbering size of the Fourth Infantry Division. The last couple years of fighting brought the fourth into the heart of Germany and it seemed like all that they were waiting on now was a surrender. The Fourth had been sent in to take and hold the town, clearing out any German defenders left. It had been a fine spring morning, and if David weren't worried about his life, he would actually have considered making the best of the day. He and the rest of his squad were sweeping down one of the city streets of the German town of Miesbach, passively placing themselves in strategic positions as they scurried along the rubble strewn streets.

The rest of the company followed suit, with only one squad ahead of David's and the other two following at the same stride as his own. They had maneuvered about a mile forward into the ruined town. Mortar rounds did not hesitate ruining any majesty this town may have once had. The classic architect style conveyed throughout most of the old town's buildings had been sundered by large craters that destroyed the buildings' infrastructure.

Up and down the street, Squad One had positioned themselves behind two sets of cars left along the side of the streets. As soon as the men had squatted down behind the abandoned cars, two rifle shots beamed off from a window above. Everyone began to take snapshots in the general direction of the oncoming fire in retaliation.

"Trouble!" Sergeant Corbin muttered.

"Where'd it come from?" Cramer up front asked.

"those two windows," Corbin said, pointing up at the set of windows that were a hundred feet down from squad one's position. "Best be careful. I bet they're packing at least submachine guns."

"we're gonna try and sneak right in front of them and throw a grenade in while Squad Three gives us some nice cover fire. Everyone else here that?" Corbin asked, assuring that the squad heard the plan he'd muttered to himself.

"Yes, Sargent!" the squad acknowledged with nodding heads.

"Good! I don't like repeatin' myself. Radio Squad Three; let 'em know about my genius plan."

Immediately after the quick confirmation with Squad Three, the small, intermittent bursts of rifle fire escalated as Squad Three began emptying their clips hastily into the side of the building where the defenders hid.

"Go! Go! Go!" Corbin shouted, waving his squad on. The soldiers rushed down the street near and in front of the house being riveted by rifle fire.

"Grenade!" Frickell, the soldier next to David yelled as he lobbed the green ball into the window above. Then followed the dramatic, suspenseful pause as the entire squad teetered on the coming, satisfying explosion.

A quick, expected rupture in the air shook everyone's eardrums, in unison with the gentle push of the blast. Gunfire from both sides ceased afterward, and Squad Three, which had previously been pinned behind the abandoned cars, hesitantly rose from cover.

"Secure that building," Corbin ordered.

The squad lined itself single file just beside the door before busting it down and storming in, rifles aimed. David followed the line of soldiers that fed into the home. It was, probably before the war, a nicer home for the area with a fairly spacious living area a bit uncommon for the homes David had seen across Germany. It would never compare to the palace of North Haven, but nothing would ever compare to a place like that. For the most part, it looked like the owners had moved out, with nothing on the hardwood floor except dust and scattered glass.

"First floor looks clear," Peterson yelled from behind a doorway that led into the kitchen.

"Copy that," Corbin remarked.

The two were not communicating by radio, but radio speak and lingo easily infected face-to-face conversation. David always liked to be clever by trying to instigate it but then cleverly pointing out how obnoxious it could be.

"What am I copying?" Frickell queried asking as innocently as he could. He even beat David to the punch.

Corbin looked back with a snarling glare, the kind of glare a man has before he's about to murder someone.

"Shut up," Corbin simply stated. The joke wasn't even that funny, but with its overuse and everyone's usual reaction, it transcended a usual joke's limits. "Where's the stairs?" Corbin asked, still sounding annoyed.

"Over here!" Peterson yelled from the kitchen.

"Did you move up yet?"

"Not yet, Sergeant!" Peterson yelled.

"All right, first floor looks clear. Let's head up top!" Corbin order.

The squad lined up in the same single file line they'd made at the door at the base of the stairs. A quick wave of Corbin's hand sent the soldiers jolting up the stairs. The upstairs was smaller, and the welcoming, wide open space of the downstairs was replaced by a narrow hall with a few doors leading off from it.

David continued up the rest of the stairs, noting that the far wall was protruding out, as if someone had tackled it.

The first soldier leading the line was Brenan, and he stopped at the first door leading down the hall, halting the momentum of the rest of the squad. He paused at the door in a moment of hesitation, which always annoyed David; Brenan always seemed to find a way to make a situation more dramatic than it already was. He slowly turned the doorknob, before bursting in with his rifle raised. A couple of the men followed him in.

David found himself now at the front of the line, moving up to cover the next door. The protruded wall brushed by him, reminding him just what room he was entering. He stopped at the door and looked at the five men behind him, giving them a quick thumbs-up before he burst into the room.

The two far windows of the room had been completely shattered, either by bullets or the explosion, and the rest of the wall around it was deranged by countless bullet holes. Six victims from the ordeal lay blasted against the walls, a bloody, unrecognizable mess, with the only traces of their identity being the iconic gray helmets and shredded gray jackets.

"Looks like they're all dead, Sarge!" David gleefully remarked. Firefights were always nasty, tedious business.

"Let me see!" Corbin said, barging by the two other men blocking the door. He looked around the room, his eyes peering over each body. "I'm only countin' six dead Germans, Private Curtis. They come in groups of ten," Korbin noted. "So, as of now, there are still four of them around."

"Maybe the other room?" Curtis commented.

"This room's clear, Sarge!" a voice shouted from the last unchecked room.

"Mmm, I'm not happy. Radio, tell the company the threat has been neutralized!"

"On it, Sergeant," the radioman, Scott, acknowledged.

"Let's go! And keep your eyes peeled; there is still trouble nearby," Corbin added.

First Squad shuffled out of the invaded home in a less dramatic fashion than they'd entered it. Third Squad had already made it up one block by the time David's squad mates had all found their way out of the home. Another squad had just positioned themselves across the street. Their squad sergeant looked over toward David's squad, pointing his finger forward.

"C'mon, c'mon, quit dillydallying; we need to go," Corbin ordered after being the last to leave the building. The squad moved up to the street corner and crouched down behind a cobblestone fence that separated someone's yard from the sidewalk.

"Who are those guys?" Frickell asked, pointing toward a couple of lingering figures peering out at them from a restaurant window.

"Civvies?" David answered. He'd seen the set of figures too. "Sarge, you see that?"

"Sure do."

"What are your orders?" Brenan inquired.

"Well, they're not our guys, and civvies should know better. So why don't you take a shot and see what happens," Corbin answered.

Brenan stared a little longer at the two figures that were now motionless before raising his rifle and firing a single shot just above the figures. Brenan's shot only put a small, obtuse crack in the window, but the return fire on the other side of it shattered the rest. A heavy torrent of light machine gun fire coming from the restaurant stippled the side of the cobblestone fence. Fortunately, the entire squad had been in good cover, each member cowering below the fence.

"Now you've done it, Brenan," Corbin remarked.

"Done what? They were going to kill us in the open!"

"Yeah, well those are probably the friends of the four that got away. Let's give 'em hell, Fourth."

The squad continued to hide behind the cobblestone fence, taking only quick, blind shots until the machine gun had, for whatever reason, stopped firing.

"Now!"

Each squad member rose and took aim at the far-off restaurant. Lingering figures in the windows seemed to flinch at the incoming fire but didn't hesitate returning the shots. Enemy fire fell around the squad, cleaving through whatever it hit. Chunks of rocks and dust exploded around their position, getting in David's eyes as he tried to fire. He hated firefights, and he always seemed to wind up in them. Third Squad had been at their far-right flank and had arrived within range to give suppressive fire. The loud clamor of a friendly Thompson submachine gun always was always a good sign.

With the support of the other squad, enemy fire had all but halted, and David was the first one to begin the advance. He jumped over the fence and began to crawl to a small crater from earlier mortar fire while maintaining fire. A figure scurried by in his crosshairs at the far wall of the building, and he took the shot. The figure fell midstride, plummeting toward the ground.

"Got 'em," David proudly remarked to himself. He crawled forward just a little closer before he realized Frickell had crawled up just to the left of him.

"Hey what's going on, Curtis?" Frickell jokingly asked.

"You know, just dying," David answered.

"Hold your fire!" Corbin yelled.

Both squads immediately stopped, realizing no fire was being returned from the building. David carefully rose to his knee, looking into the building.

"It looks clear to me, Sarge!" David yelled back. He sidled up to the building window, looked into its blasted remains, and saw no sign of life inside.

"It's clear!" David yelled back proudly.

"All right, Brenan, Curtis, Peterson, and … Frickell, go clear the building! We'll cover you," Corbin ordered.

The few called-out soldiers edged toward the building, with David waiting at the door for them.

"C'mon, ladies," David remarked, holding open the door for them.

David took two steps forward into the devastated building, slowly panning his rifle from left to right. Knocked-over tables were arranged in hopeless barricades that never had a chance at stopping the incoming mortar round that had fallen through the roof,. What had once been a quaint, little diner had been geared up and, therefore, devastated by the war it had been rigged to help stop. Brenan stood just at the entrance with Peterson behind him. The bodies of the defenders lay where they had once stood. Each had been violently knocked down and torn apart in their defense along the windowed wall.

"What was that?" Brenan asked.

David had heard it too. A boot had scraped along the ground.

"It sounded like it came from in there," David answered. He pointed toward the swinging door at the left corner of the restaurant. He lumbered closer, stepping over the makeshift barricade and keeping his crosshairs on the door, with Brenan casually following behind him.

They both positioned at opposite ends of the door. David looked Brenan in the eye and, with an affirmative nod, burst through the swinging door with his rifle aimed at whoever was on the other side. An outburst of screams followed. David quickly took in the scene—a group of civilians, from a child to grown men what looked like a German solider were huddled in the far corner of the kitchen.

"Oh, jeez." David rolled his eyes. "Let me see your hands!" he growled, pointing his rifle at the group of civilians.

They only shriveled back in fear as David took a few steps close.

"Put your hands on your heads," David demanded.

Brenan lingered behind David, and instead of threatening them all with his rifle, he gestured to them, putting his own hands on his head. The group hesitantly followed Brenan's instructions.

"Okay, come on; get up." David gestured with an upward raise of his hand.

They surprisingly understood and followed, though still hesitant, slowly rising from the asylum of the corner.

"What's going on in there?" Peterson bellowed from the doorway to the restaurant.

"We've just got some civvies. Tell Scott to radio camp for some reinforcements. We're going to have to escort 'em back," David answered.

"How many are there?" Peterson asked.

"Uh, I don't know. It looks like maybe fifteen or so."

"God damn it! Copy that," Peterson replied. David could almost hear the eye roll from the room over.

"I would think a Harvard man would be smarter than that," Brenan muttered precariously behind David.

"What are you tryna' say?" David replied skeptically, looking over his shoulder toward Brenan with a joking smile.

"I would just think a person who went to college would be able to understand that most Germans speak German, not English," Brenan jokingly added.

"Yeah well ... you could say I was teaching them," David answered. "It worked, didn't it?"

"I guess so," Brenan agreed dubiously. "So if you have a degree, why didn't you think about becoming an officer before you enlisted?"

"It was sort of a last-minute decision on my part. I just wanted to get away from my old life, and this looked like the quickest way. Besides, I don't think the army really needs an officer with a master's in business."

"True, I just don't understand why you would go about getting a college degree if you weren't even going to use it."

"Oh, I used it. But like I said, I just wanted to escape from my old life," David replied, sounding nearly wistful. "And I figured, while I'm at it, I'll teach some English to some Germans!"

They both laughed.

"I don't know why you would want to end up in a place like this. I mean you must regret it, don't you?"

"You know, I did at first. Or rather, I didn't know what I was getting into. Then I started to hate every day. And finally, I gradually accepted that I am here to stay, and whether or not I liked it didn't matter in the end, you know? I was bound to see it through till the end. I'm sure you know what I'm talkin' about." David seemed to be pondering the situation out loud.

"I do," Brenan sedately agreed.

"What about you? Why are you here?"

"Well, when I enlisted I was supposed to get a pretty good job in operations and communications."

"And?"

"They needed infantry. It's been fun though"

"Sure has," David remarked cynically, segueing their conversation into an awkward silence as David reflected upon his service in the army. Like anyone after a long trip, he just wanted to go home now.

Reinforcements had arrived to pick up where David's squad had left off. And instead of advancing farther into the city, they were on their way back to camp, escorting the civilians. The ten soldiers escorted the civilian refugees and the single German captive with his hands on his head followed by two escorts along a winding country road that led them out of town and over to their base of operations just beyond the town's outskirts. The town was practically theirs, with little pockets of resistance upon arrival. That had been quite the relief. It had been nearly two years since that initial landing at Normandy, and a year's worth of marching and fighting had brought David and the rest of the Fourth from the beaches of Normandy 750 miles east to the small town of Miesbach. The past year had been 750 miles of what felt like constant fighting. Their company had dwindled down to just half of its initial force, with even the second lieutenant getting killed in action.

The end of what felt like forever was close. The war was ending, and all everyone seemed to talk about was what they were going to do when they got home. David knew one thing was for sure; he didn't plan on staying in the army any longer than he needed to.

Of course, Thatcher was the first to stamp out any hope and spoke of an immediate redeployment over in the Pacific front after this and finishing up the war over there. He was honestly baffled he had made it this far, and he didn't want to continue pushing his luck. David never expected to die out here, just not to make it.

"Say, Fricks, what are you gonna do after the war?" David asked.

"I don't know, brother. I think I'm just gonna eat—eat somethin' that didn't come in a can," Frickell joked.

The group laughed, and even the refugees seemed to ease up a little, giving uncomfortable smiles.

"Naw, for real though," David pressed.

"I think I'm just gonna go kiss my girlfriend for the first time in two years," Frickell admitted.

"Aww, that's sweet," Peterson tone seemed almost envious.

"How 'bout the rest of you?! Word is we might be getting out of here soon, so I need some ideas," David exclaimed.

"I don't know. I might just stay in, maybe," Brenan answered carefully.

"That's a terrible idea, Brenan! Why would you even bring that up?" David joked.

"I just can't wait for a shower! I'm pretty sure there is still sand in my shoes from Normandy!" David explained "Maybe followed by a cigar and a nice drink and my life will be set."

"Hey, David, didn't you say you have a wife and kids waiting back home for you?" Peterson interrupted.

"Yeah, I guess so …"

"Then why wouldn't that be the first thing you do?" Peterson pressed.

"I don't know. It wasn't what I had in mind … I was thinking something more fun…."

The other men began to all start talking about home again, and once it started, it never stopped. David usually joined in, but Peterson had brought up that nagging, wishful notion of what he really wanted to do when he got back home. He missed his wife and his kids, and he'd never understood—not until this point, when life had been boiled down to mere perseverance—what they meant to him. Moreover, he understood that he had founded his world upon debauchery and that was never really there to support him. David had known that what he'd done was wrong the moment he'd hit her, and the passage of time had probably only festered and worsened the matter. Every time he thought of what had happened, it had hung over his head as a looming premonition that one day he would need to confront.

The small, bustling camp two miles out of town could hardly contain the bustling action within it. Between the movement of trucks and boots, the ground had been tilled to mud beneath it all. Pointed tents stretched all along the camp in the perfect rows, with the bustle of soldiers filling in the spaces between the lines.

David's squad had marched just up to the camp's borderline when they received the pleasant welcome of Sergeant Thatcher with his invariable frown smoking a cigarette.

"Oh, what the fuck! You can't bring all of them in here!" Thatcher protested, a mouthful of cigarette choking his words.

"Sorry, Sergeant, command's orders are to process all the civilians here," Corbin retorted.

"Who the fuck do you think I am? I am command!"

"Sorry, Sergeant, all the officers who are above you said so," Korbin added.

"Oh don't even get me started on them!" Thatcher yelled in a deep, monotonous timbre. "Well, I have some good news," Thatcher added.

Everyone's eyes were now fixed on Thatcher, each man hoping for the expected news that they would be withdrawing.

"We're being relieved and placed on occupation duty here. Welcome to your new home for I don't know how long."

"So we're not going home?" Frickell asked, disenchanted now by the good news.

"Nope. Just means we're not going to get shot at as much," Thatcher replied.

A shared look of disappointment swept over the squad.

"Will you cheer up, ya knuckleheads! The war is almost over, and command won't keep us here any longer than they have to. We're almost done!" Thatcher added in with the most optimistic voice David had ever heard from him.

Everyone's face brightened up a little, but Thatcher's words didn't change the fact that they were still stuck here.

"All right, c'mon. Bring them in for processing. And quit moping around." Thatcher pointed his thumb back toward the camp.

Everyone marched into the camp that would soon host the prologue to their deployment.

CHAPTER 20

The Reconciliation
of Ghosts

David curved his car around the winding switchbacks leading deep into the mountains. It had been years since he'd traveled this road. He had only been back in the United States for a few days, but he had finally figured out the one thing he wanted to do when he got home. Two years of training and another four in Europe, all away from his family and his life, had led him to this point. The road straightened out as it traveled just along the opening of the valley that held North Haven. The towering, gray monolith was a welcoming sight for David. It had been home a long time ago, and it stood just as tall as it had when he'd left it. The castles of Europe were merely shadowed by North Haven's size.

He pulled up the entrance road, past the estate's walls, and up into the side entrance driveway. The distance between the walls and the estate's boundaries had obscured all the most recent flaws of the estate that later became apparent to David as he drove up to the door; the white gravel driveway was washed out and hardly any of it was left, windows were streaked and even the once bright red door that used to welcome all guests to North Haven had faded to be lackluster and mute. It wasn't at all what it used to be and to David, it had been stripped of its dignity.

He walked up to the door, proudly sporting his army uniform, decorated with the myriad pins he had earned during the war. His knapsack, brimming with his life that he managed to keep over the past six years, was slung over his shoulder. The large, intimidating door into the castle made David belittled in his stance. He took a deep breath in an attempt to muster all of the courage he'd found within him over the past few years.

He knocked, listening to the sound of his beckoning dissipate into the void of the home. There was no response. No one was ever going to hear his vain knock. Back when Eugene had owned the home, he had hired an attendant just to stand watch at the door. But even David had done away with that policy as soon as Eugene had passed away. He stared helplessly, wondering how he would ever be heard. He tried one more time, with the same reply: silence.

David traveled around the side of the building, headed for the seldom-used main entrance at the center of the estate. He walked in the garden, where sprouts and leaves crowded the path. The rest of the garden followed suit, poorly managed—not ignored, just neglected. He started to question whether anyone even lived here still. The home's most prominent characteristic—its seclusion from the rest of the world—may have led it to a place forgotten in history. David made his way up the exaggerated steps leading to the main door and tried knocking against it as loudly as he could.

He was almost certain no one lived here anymore. The door remained motionless as he stared at it, hoping for someone to come. He looked down with a heavy sigh, realizing he had probably missed the last chance he would ever get to see his wife and children again. And by some gracious miracle, the door opened and Jack's wife, Violet, stuck her head, beguiled by the strange knocker. As soon as the mysterious knocker lifted his head in surprise, Violet's face fell to a pale white.

"David," Violet stuttered.

"Hello, Violet," David responded awkwardly.

"What are you doing here? We thought you left … for good," Violet asked, still stunned.

"I guess you could say I got a little homesick," he joked, pointing toward his uniform. "Can I come in?"

"Of course, of course, please come in." She gestured inside, fully opening the door.

David stepped into North Haven for the first time in six years. Wistful memories became reality once again as he looked around. And after nostalgia sunk in, David took another look, seeing just how empty the home had become. The brilliant chandelier in its center remained dim, casting a dull darkness throughout the wing. Furniture that had once lined and filled the walls and corners was replaced by vacant space. The home had fallen far from its initial whimsical existence to what felt like a decrepit hollow that mourned for its own disposition.

"Violet, what happened to the furniture?" David asked quizzically.

"Well, David, when you left, the budget got a little tight. So we sold what we didn't need," she answered solemnly, as if regretful.

David nodded but was stunned to see the home like this.

"So who is home?" David asked, curious to hear about Jessica and the kids. He was afraid to mention them specifically, not wanting to hint to his atrocious past.

"Just me, Jack, and our kids. Oh, and Robert. David, if you'd like, you can stay for supper," she offered, sounding almost intimidated by the offer.

"I would love to, Violet. Thank you,"

"Violet, who is that at the door?" a stern voice echoed from up the stairs. Jack looked down from the upstairs balcony with supervising eyes.

"Look, Jack; it's David!" Violet answered.

"What!" Jack replied, confused. "David. What is he doing here?"

"I just wanted to come back home," David replied, stopping Violet before she could answer.

Jack looked down at David with an unwelcoming face. He stepped down the stairs and walked up to his brother-in-law, glaring at him straight in the eye, unflinching in his stride. "Well then … Welcome home," Jack said in the most unconvincing manner. He had extended his hand to shake David's.

David gleefully shook it with a smile. David knew he wasn't welcome and knew he could never fix the past. But at least he could amend the current animosity between them. "I'm so happy to be home."

"David will be staying with us for dinner. Do you need a place to sleep too?" Violet was telling Jack before she asked David about his plans for the night.

"Oh I couldn't—" David responded.

"Oh, come on. You've helped us out all those years. This is the least we can do!" Jack interrupted, sounding patronizing. "You wanted to come home, and home is here!"

"Thanks," David responded.

"I'll tell Martha to ready the guest room. Supper will be ready at five!" Violet responded before dashing off to the west wing. "And, David … Make yourself at home."

"I will. Thank you." He nodded with a smile.

"Here, let me show you to your room." Jack gestured to the upstairs.

The two traveled through the hallowed halls of North Haven. Jack led David into the one of the far-off halls of the guest wing, or what used to be the guest wing. The doors to all the rooms were closed, but David knew only empty space stood on the other side. There was Jessica's old room, conspicuously hidden among the rest of the doors; his office just down from her old room; and right next to it, the room they'd shared together. These rooms had all the details he had remembered but seemed only a faint outline of what they once had been. It was all like an old friend had once lived here but had moved away, and all that were left were the scant details of what was left of him. Maybe David had just been expecting too much.

"Here, 203. There aren't any bedsheets or anything, but Martha will fix that," Jack said, handing David a small key carrying the same number. "I'll, uh, be in my office if you need anything," Jack added before escaping.

After David knew he was alone, he breathed a humiliating sigh of relief looking at the comfort to be had behind the door to his room. He opened the door to one of the last quaint, little guest rooms at North Haven. All that was left in it was a bed and dresser to its side, but he didn't care. He closed the door behind him and dropped the bag where he stood as he gaped at the comfortable king-sized mattress. He didn't care about the sheets and instead just crashed horizontally across the bed with his feet hanging off the edge, rewarding himself with a nap after a long six years.

*　　*　　*

"Umm, Mr. Curtis, sir." David felt a gentle, tap on his back.

David turned around, uttering sleep-induced nonsense before realizing that he had fallen asleep. A young, brunette maid was standing next to the bed attempting to get his attention.

"Mr. Curtis, dinner is almost ready," she announced monotonously, still staring over him.

"Oh shoot!" David got up, squinting, and dashed out of his room still wearing the army uniform he'd inadvertently slept in.

Daylight had dimmed as the sun had fallen behind the distant fault line of the horizon. David scurried down the halls, lit in phosphorescent shades of orange and yellow by the falling sun. A few of the lights that lined the hallway had been carefully selected and lit to make up for the loss of daylight. He cursed himself the entire way to the dining room for sleeping in. On his way down, David had expected to run into a few friendly faces just as he always had. No one was to be found.

He skidded through one of the interloping passages into the main hall and dashed into the main wing, finally reaching the dining hall. Jack sat alone at the head of the table reading last week's paper.

"What are you doing?" Jack asked suspiciously.

"I thought dinner was ready," he stuttered, realizing he'd mistaken the maid's words.

"No. It'll be ready in about fifteen minutes," Jack answered. "By the way, what's with the uniform?"

"Oh," David looked down, realizing he was still wearing his uniform. "I was in the army."

Jack continued to look at him, perplexed.

"I just got back from Germany," David added, pointing in whatever random direction was behind him.

"I mean why are you still wearing it. Isn't there anything less…" Jack thought of his next words carefully with conceited grin. "… starchy you could wear?"

David suddenly became aware of how itchy and stiff he was after passing out for hours in his dress uniform. He adjusted his collar as if it would help. "You're right." He added with a nervous laugh. "I did pack something more comfortable. I'm going to go ahead and change into that!" David added as Jack dismissed him a snap of his newspaper as he turned the page.

Casually passing through one of the halls, he came upon the room where he had spent his last moments in North Haven. He stopped to somberly stare at the monument to his mistakes. All he could do was shake his head in regret at the door leading into the room where he'd hit her. All the things that had led up to that moment he could never imagine doing now, and as he looked back now, they all seemed like someone else's atrocious actions that David was now responsible for.

After he changed, David headed back to the dining room, where he found the table covered from edge to edge in silverware and platters of food. David's eyes broadened at the site of so much homemade food. Jack, Robert, and Violet were all at the head, with three children who David hardly recognized, Jack's kids, right beside them. Sally didn't even recognize him. But Michael and Jeffery seemed eerily wary and simply stared at him when he wasn't looking. He carefully took a seat next to Michael, trying not to disrupt their daily ritual any further.

"Hi, Michael," David said timidly, looking down at the boy with a friendly smile.

"Hi…" Michael replied in a shrilled voice.

David returned his gaze to the food with a disconcerted look. He was just an unwelcome stranger in his old home.

"You know, kids, David just got back from the last Great War," Jack mentioned, with a slight hint of his typical patronization back.

"What was it like, David?" Violet asked eagerly.

"Yeah, what was it like?" Jack encouraged, baiting David into some sort of argument.

David knew what Jack was trying to do, but once the steady flow of memories began, he couldn't help but smile to himself and talk about it. "There was a whole lot of marching," David said to himself with a little chuckle. "And whole lotta complaining 'bout it."

David went on through dinner, telling of his seven hundred-mile march across Europe and how he had survived every step of the way. He told them of the men he'd followed along the way and what they had said and their stories. He talked about how he'd had fought alongside and nearly died with those men through the battles and countless firefights that had tried to end their march. And, inadvertently, he revealed to them how he had cast his demons out, changing from the selfish coward who had quivered on the beaches of Normandy to who he was today—an upright man telling tales of his righteous victory and the sacrifice he'd endured over for the past four years.

They all stared at him, daring only taking bites during pauses in the story, as David recalled and retold all of the epic accounts of bravery he had seen or had been forced into.

"Well, it sounds like you've been through a lot these past years," Jack began.

David could already foresee the demeaning comment coming.

"So, you ought to rest up. I don't know what your plans will be in the years to come, but you're always welcome here. After all, it is *partly* your home."

"Thanks for the offer, but I'll probably be heading out by tomorrow. I'm looking for someone," David said, hoping someone would ask him who. But no one did, and he wasn't brave enough to ask where Jessica was, not after what he'd done.

After dinner, David talked a little while longer, catching up with the other part of the family that he realized he hadn't missed until now. Jack had become somewhat of a successful bond man. Violet and the kids were getting along well, with the kids being shipped off to school through the weeks and coming home for vacations and weekends.

But before David could ask Robert how he'd been, Robert had vanished, receding back into the walls of North Haven immediately after dinner.

* * *

Just before midnight, David took one last tour of North Haven, as he realized this might be his last time here. The home that had initially captivated him had remained the same to this day. Extending facets and features intertwined, enlaced with fantastic details that had always made this place feel like more than just a home. This had been where he'd met his wife, where he'd conducted his business, and where he'd spent his time of rest. But seeing it now, he realized this place had never really taught him anything. It had always been too elaborate to be just a home, and it had taken many days away from this paradise to correct his ways.

His tour finally ended at his room, the room where he was staying. He unlocked the door; crashed on the comfy, now sheeted bed, and looked up at the ceiling, just thinking about the promise of tomorrow that was no longer threatened, before he slipped into sleep.

CHAPTER 21

The Noose

David woke up feeling a throbbing pain in the back of his head. A sack had been tied around his face, letting in only the diminished gray light of the morning. His arms and legs were bound by rope to a chair. A cool morning breeze whipped around his exposed legs. He looked around in a panic, not knowing where he was, and from what he could tell, he was alone. A few hesitant footsteps shuffled around him and toward his right.

"Who are you?" David wailed. "What is going on?"

The footsteps didn't respond, and David sat in silence, trying to breath. Despite not being able to see, he looked around in a panic. To his right, he heard the person moving again. David quickly looked over to his right, the sack on his head expanding and contracting rapidly in time with his breathing. What sounded like a strong knot being tightened on a rope followed.

"What are you doing? What's going on?" David howled.

The figure walked behind him and then took a few steps upward until it was above David. He heard the harsh tightening of the rope again. The figure stepped down and stood in front of

182

David. The eclipse of his shadow loomed over David's head as it hesitated to make its next move.

David's head yanked forward as the bag had been violently ripped off. David looked up now to see his captor. Jack domineered above him, looking down upon David with a vengeful look, swollen by fear and uncertainty.

"Jack!" David cried out, smiling in recognition, and feeling the rapturous comfort of safety. "What are you doing?"

"What does it look like I'm doing?" he shot back, pointing up above David.

David looked up to see a looped knot dangling precariously close to his neck.

"Jack, what are you doing?" David asked again, letting out a distressed chuckle.

Jack cackled a harsh, dry, forced laugh. "What does it look I'm doing?" he repeated.

"But why?" David asked innocently.

"Are you seriously asking that? This is for everything you've done to me and my family."

"What have I done?" David pressed.

"You were the one who split up our family and left us out here without money to tend to this burden! Then you had the nerve to come back here, spouting about how much of a hero you were!" Jack cried violently. He yelled it as if repeating a hateful mantra that he'd followed over the past six years.

David closed his eyes, feeling a repressed guilt come back to him. "Jack, I don't understand! I've committed no crime worthy of hanging ... Jack, please don't do this."

"Just shut up!" Jack yelled back. He walked behind David and brought the rope around his neck. His entire body carried a distressed but determined look. Jack was no psychopath, and with every step he took, he hesitated, only to be carried forward by a spiteful oath he held himself to.

"Jack, don't do this. I'm sorry. I didn't know I could have done this much damage. I came back to make up for what I've done."

"There is nothing you can do to fix that," Jack muttered, fixing the loop around David's neck.

"Just at least tell me Jessica and the kids are doing okay," David asked.

Jack paused for a moment before bursting into laughter. "You don't know, do you?" Jack managed to yell in between bouts of laughter. "Jessica is dead, and your kids have been kidnapped by your beloved Judith."

"What? What do you mean she's dead? And the kids ... gone?" David could barely mumble now, taken by the unfathomable grief that his family was gone and there was nothing he could do to atone for what he had done. Even now, he felt selfish, realizing he'd come back for redemption first and had put his family second.

"I knew I should've stopped you that night," Jack muttered to himself. "Doctor said she hit her head on the floor hard enough, and that did it. Just that ..." Jack swallowed. "Police have been looking for you all this time, but you've just been hiding at the other end of the world—a war hero!" he shouted sarcastically. "Spare me; you're just a murderer." He smiled maniacally, as if the declaration justified his action.

David wasn't listening. His eyes stared expressionless into the ground in front of him, recalling the last moment he'd had with his wife. She'd died trying to for his love and attention, and he'd struck her down.

"Jessica, I'm so sorry," David whispered, hoping by some divine joke that maybe someday she could hear it. "Jack, I'm sorry. I guess I understand now," David said, his tone stronger.

Jack remained motionless, standing behind David. David was gripping onto the seat and closing his eyes, bracing himself for whatever was to come. He heard Jack slowly step backward, indecisive with every step. David closed his eyes and leaned as comfortably back in the chair as he could, waiting for the choking tug of the noose.

CHAPTER 22

Ghost Maker

R obert stood at the railing in the side foyer of the home, watching as laborers moved the last of the furniture out of North Haven. Jack came out from the entrance below him, limping along with an oversized suitcase toward the entrance. A week ago, just after David's abrupt arrival and elusive departure, Jack had said he wanted to move. Robert had never seen Jack so convinced about anything in his life. His brother's only response as to why he wanted to move was that he was done with this place and it was time to move. Jack offered no talk of family responsibility; nor did he even say anything about selling North Haven. Robert had other plans.

Jack waddled over to the foyer door as he managed his suitcase in one hand and looked up at Robert, who stood perched leaning over the balcony rail looking down upon Jack.

"C'mon, Robert. What are you doing? We're leaving today!" Jack yelled up to Robert, who refused to give in to Jack's demands. Jack glared up at his brother, shaking his head before waddling out the door to his car.

Robert had refused to follow along with Jack's spontaneous urge to move away from the place he'd lived his whole life. He watched Jack walk back in and start heading upstairs toward Robert, who continued to stare blankly over the foyer.

"Robert, what has gotten into you?" Jack sneered. "There is nothing for you here! You need to move out like the rest of us."

"I can't leave my whole life behind, Jack." Robert contested, trying to ignore the obvious facts.

A laborer walked up behind Jack, tapping his shoulder. "Umm, boss, we can't open one of the rooms you told us to pack up—the one in the upper east hall; it's locked," the laborer said.

"Just leave it then," Jack replied bitterly. He glanced over at Robert, who had tried to ignore the interruption by fixating on the foyer that, along with the rest of the home, embodied every sentiment he had ever known. "What the hell do you think you're doing?" Jack demanded.

"I told you; I am not leaving," Robert declared.

Jack sighed, glaring at Robert with a scornful look. Robert continued ignoring him as Jack stormed off back down the stairs. With Jack gone, Robert let go of his stern fixation. He retreated from his uncompromising stance and moved back down toward his family. He had no idea how he was going to manage to live up here by himself. He'd managed to keep several thousand dollars locked away that had been left to him by his father's will, and that would last him a lifetime. But he felt something else was missing from North Haven, and a lingering temptation and uncertainty tugged at him, suggesting that he might be wrong, that maybe he should leave. Robert continued to stare amicably out toward the marble foyer, waiting for Jack to say his goodbye.

The laborers continued for the next twenty minutes, packing up whatever furniture was left, except for what was in Robert's room and the guest room, which, for whatever reason, Jack decided to leave. Then, making one final trip out to their van, the laborers never came back in. They took off in their van and headed straight to Manhattan, Jack's new home. Robert solemnly watched as Jack shuffled his family out toward the exit. By the time they neared the door, Robert briskly walked down the stairs and toward the exit. Jack stopped upon hearing his brother's footsteps and turned around with an oddly pensive look.

"Did you change your mind?" Jack asked, looking back at Robert, who stood expressionless in the doorway.

"No, I just wanted to say good-bye," Robert said monotonously, trying to remain stoic.

"Robert, nothing good ever came out of this place. Why would you want to stay?" Jack asked.

"It's been my life, and I couldn't just leave it so suddenly and on such baseless reasons," Robert said. "I don't even understand why you're leaving."

As Jack took one last look at his brother and with it, he left with a somber, wordless good-bye and shut the door behind him. Robert stood in the doorway, lost for any understanding as his remaining family disappeared from his life. He opened the door, hoping to say good-bye to his brother. But Jack had already left leaving on the receding rumble of his car heading down the mountain.

From the door, Robert could see the road recede into the woods and even farther as it escaped across into the horizon. For Robert, the broad world outside North Haven had been narrowed down into that doorframe, and from that single vista, he had wondered why anyone would want to leave. Robert turned around and looked back into the wild expanse of North Haven. Halls stretched in every which way, unable to define his vast, empty domain. He stared outward, trying to see the end of his boundless new home, broadened by its labyrinth of halls and filled with the intimidating silence of solitude. He smiled hopelessly back toward his home, wondering what to do with his void.

Robert began to recede back into home but the nagging sight of his old mailbox, inlaid within the wall next to the entrance stopped him. Robert had kept his pledge for years never to open it, regardless of how much it had constantly teased of hope. Robert knew what was inside, and he didn't want to confront it.

He remembered back to the day after he'd made that pledge. It was Dr. Taft, in his makeshift classroom there at North Haven, who had told Robert something that had stuck with him all these years. He had been stapled to his chair in, trying to keep his mind off of her and whatever had gone wrong.

"Is there a reason the Civil War doesn't have you at the edge of your seat, boy?" Dr. Taft shrewdly asked.

Robert had remained inclined in his seat, lost in some thought or another about the incident. "Sorry, doctor, just thinking about other things."

"You're always thinking about that girl. And before, you'd smile deliriously to yourself about this girl who, frankly, I don't believe exists, forcing me to put up with that stupid, naive grin. Now you're just all mopey and broken."

Robert paid Taft no mind and continued to stare expressionlessly toward the board.

Taft sighed and walked over to Robert's desk. He kneeled down. "Listen, I, uh, don't know what happened between you two. But it's obvious that she meant a lot to you. I had loved someone, once and it was the biggest, most unavoidable mistake that I ever made. But, Robert, love will be one of those mistakes that you'll regret everything about, except for loving that person, and you'll probably make that mistake again." Dr. Taft laid his hand gently on Robert's shoulder.

Robert had found no definite solace in his tutor's words. At the time, he didn't believe he had made a mistake. But looking back now, he saw that his love was a regret he didn't want to live with. It was immaturity that had forced him to believe there was hope for his and Sierra's detached relationship. Robert looked away from the mailbox, liking to believe that he was past that point in his life.

*   *   *

Weeks passed after Robert's self-sentence to solitude. Robert spent this time doing what he had always done. He read the countless undefined-genre of books that chocked the shelves of his father's libraries. The myriad of books that had been bought only for show had finally been used for their intended purposes. On the days when reading lost its pleasure, Robert would try and listen to the old radio he had kept in his room. But after Jack left, Robert was only haunted by the voices coming from outside North Haven and tried to avoid it to convince himself he had made the right decision in staying.

He had always thought being alone and doing exactly this was what he wanted, but he could never convince himself he had made the right decision. The familiarity he had clung to had decayed into a hounding silence that persisted through every attempt he made to ignore it.

The home's hallowed walls echoed only that insufferable silence. Its architecture had become twisted and hollowed beyond anything he could remember, now standing only as vast, hollow vestiges of his past that he tried to live in. He had lived his entire life in solitude. Why now did it bother him?

Every day, he would walk the halls, no longer wandering but searching the home that he lived in. Its fall from grace left it colorless and shameful, and Robert was searching for its true glory. When he never found it, he wondered if his father's testament to his personal success had all but become a ruin. On this particular day, Robert went down the west wing's main hall, carelessly meandering around before being stopped by the door leading to the auditorium. He'd always admired his father's idea—"Why not bring the shows to us!" But there had never been a single show played in North Haven. The only memorable thing that ever happened in that auditorium were games of hide-and-seek with his nieces and nephews. Robert opened the door farther, following the memories. He flicked on the light and looked out at the empty rows of seats, laughing to himself and remembering all those times. It was remembering those little moments that forced him to remember he couldn't leave that behind. The home had already lost so much, and seeing what little details had survived, Robert felt dedicated to staying with it and saving it from further decimation.

He looked to the stage and beyond it and felt the welcoming of nostalgia push him farther into the theatre. The brick wall that had once been covered by the stage screen stood exposed now, flaunting its crudity in the eloquent theater. A door stood in the center of the wall—a door Robert had nearly forgotten about.

He climbed up on the stage, anticipating the wistful memories that lay beyond that door. It led to a small service tunnel that branched out, leading in both directions to two different rooms. He walked down toward the left most room, expecting what he remembered, and opening the door to the unwelcoming surprise that his old paradise had fallen along with the rest of the home. It was now an old boiler room, cluttered with rusted metal shelving atop which stood miscellaneous cans and tools. Robert stumbled into the room, wondering what he had been expecting, and looked past one of the shelves to see the faint outlining of chalk he and Rachael drawn together six years earlier.

That precious, unrecognized moment had been the last time he'd ever spent time with Rachael before Judith had run off with the little girl. The place where he had his last conversation with his sister. He had told her to risk everything for her love because he'd regretted never doing the same. He smirked, feeling thankful that at least he'd made that last moment meaningful despite knowing that he'd never been a good brother or uncle. He'd chosen to remove himself from them all now, and he castigated himself for doing so—reflecting on the regretful drawbacks of his past self-inflicted solitude.

So much seemed to have happened in such a forgetful room. He let his hand stray across the top of the piano, trying to feel what the past had left behind. The piano was really why he'd come here. The small piano he'd spent hours a day on remained hidden, tucked away behind a shelf. He'd always imagined that it belonged to a servant. But no one had ever claimed it, and Robert guessed that, since he was the last one left, it was his. He pulled it out from behind the shelving under the restraint of its rusted metal wheels and grinned at the old, familiar sight. Playing the piano had been an old habit, killed by personal negligence. One day, he had just stopped playing.

He peered over the piano with a satisfying, nostalgic grin and removed the dusted cover, revealing the pale and cracked keys. He ran his hand over each one before playing a random C note. He flinched at the tone. It needed tuning. On the shelf the piano hid behind it stood a stack of sheet music he used to play through. He looked through the pages, smiling wistfully at all his old favorites. As he searched through the pile he stumbled upon a few crumpled, stained pages that hid at the bottom of the stack—the song he'd been writing for Sierra.

He looked down at it with a somber gaze, trying to remind himself that he'd moved past it. But he couldn't resist his curiosity, his desire to play his dreaded past, and he reached over to the piano, playing out each note. The neglected piano sounded an off-key version of the bygone melody he'd written. He pulled up the rusted workbench stool he used to sit on while he played and followed along to the clever melody he'd written years ago.

The song pulled him back into a faded memory of the golden years of his life—the years that had been refined into this charming melody. The song abruptly ended in the middle of the second page, forty-third measure. Robert smiled vaingloriously at the small stack of pages in front of him, realizing his own cleverness. It stumbled in rhythm in some areas, but nothing was ever perfect when you were reading a draft. He began altering the rhythm as he played the original piece so that he might fix the past.

A few minutes into his composition, he stopped, realizing he could finally play the ballroom grand piano without having anyone hear him. He leapt from the stool, grabbing the sheets, and jolted off eager to finally be able to appreciate his solitude.

In Robert's mind, the doors to the ballroom had been shut for nearly a decade and a thick layer of dust had sealed the door off. It had probably been opened for cleaning and maintenance, but the room had never been properly used since Eugene died. When that happened, the influx of guests dropped to nothing, with David or Jack constantly rejecting any unsolicited visitors who arrived at the doors asking about any parties. Robert didn't mind that. It always looked bigger when it was empty.

The vaulted expanse that led up to a stage on the opposite end remained as he remembered it, empty. And although designed to be filled wih tables and chairs along with a crowd, it had only one permanet fixture; the lone piano still left atop of the stage. He walked across the hall, recalling every splendid memory he'd once had here and forced to accept the debilitating disappointment that he would never relive anything quite like it. Guests who'd formerly mingled in the corners enclosing the dancers who lingered on the center floor had left no mark, and only the floor they once stood on remained.

He lurched over to the grand piano—one thing that hadn't seemed to fade with time. But it was also the thing he could hardly remember. He pressed one of the pristine, white keys, and a finely tuned note rang out, reflecting the quality and craftsmanship that he had been denied his entire time in North Haven.

Sporadic and random notes echoed across the empty ballroom hall for no one to hear, forming a melody that adjusted itself through each play through. It echoed farther into Robert's mind, unsettling the past, forgotten thoughts that had become distorted by his own nostalgia. As he played, he wrote down what he liked and decided he ought to finish the piece. Robert believed that all that he had added to the old draft flowed seamlessly, measure to measure, and he felt the finished piece to be a perfect ode to his time here. It then became apparent to Robert that maybe this was his fate; destined to stay here until he finished this one song and with it become one of the great musical composers of his time. He would be known by everyone. And with the thought of everyone, Sierra slipped in, and he shook his head. He didn't want to care about her. He was writing this for personal gain, not for her anymore.

When the force driving his inspiration exhausted itself upon the two added sheets to the old manuscript, he proudly looked down at the draft pages he had written and walked away, feeling accomplished and proud of every decision he'd made that had led him to this point.

The next day, after motivating himself to wake up for an early start, he glanced over at the previous day's work, played, and played it in distaste. The upbeat, smooth flow of the original melody had unintentionally segued into a bereft, downtrodden dirge. He crumpled up yesterday's progress and brought out a new sheet of paper. Hours of composing and recomposing followed and with it, Robert felt that he had outdone himself again with today's progress belittling whatever he did yesterday.

The days that followed afterword followed the same routine, subtly diminishing the importance of what he did. He would end the day composing something that would sound ingenious and original and inevitably find it to be trite and melancholy the following morning pressing Robert to throw away yesterday's progress. So what had originated as a blissful reminder of the past slowly degenerated into a visceral burden that caused Robert to realize the decrepit palace he chose to live in. Worst of all, it brought up the nagging reason Robert had started the song in the first place.

Those nagging thoughts that Robert had dwelled upon for days after he'd given up on Sierra had returned full circle to heckle him and haunt him again. Memories of Sierra took his attention away from his work as he indulged in the past and was quick to punish himself for it. It was easier for him to think about what could have been than to move past it. Only a couple days after he started his work, Robert would sit at the piano stopped in thought of his song and taken away by thoughts of her. Their derisiveness distracted him from anything else he tried to do.

Three weeks after Robert had begun augmenting the old love song he'd found, he built another small monument to his daily defeat. A small mound of crumpled papers lay right next to the piano. He sat down uneasily next to his monument of defeat and tried to compose. He played the high, ecstatic notes that ended the original piece and, like always, segued downward into a slow, deliberate burn in the melody. He kept playing the same original variation of notes, as he had done for the last few days, finding this to be the only way to play the song. But he was never content with the theme, unfit to be a masterpiece. His hands lifted from the keyboard and wrote down the played notes, but he stopped himself in the middle of a pen stride, trying to escape the ritualistic defeat he subjected himself to daily. He waited for the lurking whisper that would remind him of her—the way she had left him with only letters and, in the end, not even that. The piano shook as he stood up, shaken by the grief and anger that he should have felt years ago.

He went upstairs, back to his room to reread the letters she had sent him. None of them foretold of the absence of the tenth letter, and Robert couldn't bear to read them again. It should have been up to him to end it, after the first letter.

He slid the letters under his bed, realizing where he was. Everything that had mattered to him had been lost, and he had neglected that truth all this time, praising only the sparse few good memories. The actions of his past and those of others, moment for moment, had led him to this forsaken point, and his misery had ultimately been his decision all along. He held his face in his hands, hiding himself from this humiliating realization, feeling foolish for having pushed himself away from all those he had ever loved and having belittled his own life by contentiously exerting attention on the things that never really mattered in the end. He had ensconced himself, to be free from the judgment and change of the world but had abandoned everything by doing so. This house never was his family or his life; and back then, Sierra was neither. But until this point, he had believed she was.

Robert ran down to the main hall with all the money he had left, bound to let himself out of the trap he had put himself in all these years. He pushed through the main hall's front door to the wild expanse of North Haven's front lawn and made his way to the main gate, which he had just remembered didn't even have a road leading up to it. The gate protested and groaned as Robert pushed it as far as its rusted hinges would turn. Robert stared out into the woods, forcing himself not to look back at North Haven, and slipped through the gate to what he knew would be a better life.

CHAPTER 23

Elegies for Misbegotten Glory

Jordan searched the rest of David's room, finding nothing personal except for what was in his knapsack. She let out a heavy sigh, for her trip here had proven to be pointless. She could continue to scour every crevice of the home, but she knew the owners had left nothing identifiable behind. She was out of supplies, and she would have to return home. She rubbed her eyes, trying to keep from falling asleep, and slipped Curtis's dog tag into her pocket. Her stay here was only supposed to last till this morning, before she was to hike back down toward civilization; instead the afternoon sun hung high overhead, and she probably wouldn't be home till tomorrow.

Jordan left Curtis's room and navigated her way back to the room she was staying in. She had gotten pretty good at maneuvering through the home's expansive interior. Nothing was ever familiar, though. The crumbling walls shied away any feeling of comfort or consistency. All it really was were empty halls that filled the spaces between the grand facade of a palace that seemed to offer so much promise but, upon further investigation, proved to be nothing more than pomp and shallowness The home was connected to nothing and had nothing left to witness but its own destruction. A monument deemed by the rest of mankind not worthy of remembering.

There was never doubt in Jordan's mind that something had happened here. But whatever had happened had been forgotten. Whatever past glory or anguish the past owners had endured no longer mattered. The past was forgiving because it is forgetting. Likely, no one remembered anything about this place, and any memories that had once existed had been liberated or consigned to oblivion. Regardless of how wavering or interesting the life of anything might be, all life eventually met with the same scheduled end. Nothing remained of the home's life, as if such a lavish thing had been cast away to crumble to time.

Jordan reached her room and grabbed the one notebook that she had filled with notes. She'd expected more, but this was good enough for her. Along with the notebook, she grabbed Robert's letters and the piano music that she'd found in the ballroom. She remembered the first time she'd seen the house extending across the distant horizon. Maybe she had just hoped for too much. She packed up her living quarters and compressed all her belongings into the massive backpack that she would have to carry for the next ten hours. Time beckoned, and she didn't want to be stranded out in the woods in the dark. She scurried out of her room and headed down toward the side foyer, where the dirt road leading out of the estate began. She didn't know what would happen to the home and doubted that she would ever come back.

The side foyer basked in the same diminished light as it had the day she'd arrived. Balancing her backpack, she carefully stepped down the spiraling steps leading to the first floor. From the high vantage of the steps, she saw something that had eluded her before—a mail drop box that she had almost left unchecked. Her previously careful steps turned into a delighted dash toward the mailboxes that she knew would probably be a disappointment. Six columns by four rows of mailboxes had been set up on a side wall near the entrance. Only the top six had names—Eugene, Pearl, Jessica, Jack, Robert, and David—a little monument to those who had once lived here; the rest were numbered.

Jordan pulled out her notebook and quickly jotted down the names before pulling out a small crowbar to pry open the mailboxes. The familiar name of Robert cried out to be opened first, and so Jordan slid the crowbar into the small side of the mailbox. And with a painful crack, the lock gave way, opening the door. Jordan took a step back from the recoil of her force followed by a compensating step forward to look inside the mailbox. It was empty. Jordan stared for a while inside, but nothing ever showed itself. She took a step back knowing nothing was left to check.

A surging wind interrupted the moment. It wailed through the home, moving in and out of the rafters and singing out a moan, a mournful elegy to the ruins of the home, despite the wind furthering the home's demise. She turned her back on the home, knowing not what had transpired in the past, only that whatever had been no longer carried on here.

Printed in the United States
By Bookmasters